# First, Do Harm
## Donna Lorenz Motta

*But his anger is just for a moment. And his favor is for a lifetime. Weeping may tarry from the night. But joy comes with the morning.*

*Psalm 30:5*

Dedication
To my mother. With love.

Copyright 2019@All Rights Reserved

## Copyright & Legal Information

are purely used for clarification purposes and no owners are in any way affiliated with this work.

# CHAPTER 1

"Your father is sick."

Danny Oxman sensed his father was *really* sick by his mother's expression; eyes squinty; jaw contorting.

"What happened? Isn't papa at work?" Danny said, looking up from his third-grade math book.

"No. He's in hospital. Uncle Ben is on his way to take us," Miriam said, glancing out the window. "Oh, here he is now. Let's go!"

Miriam untied the strings of her full body apron, and they left the house. Danny noticed his mother failed to lock the door behind them, but decided not to say anything.

Miriam slipped into the front seat of Uncle Ben's Ford Model T while Danny got into the back next to his Cousin Ronnie, who was two years older than him.

"Hey," Ronnie said, banging the soles of his shoes against the back of the driver's seat.

"Stop that!" Uncle Ben snapped.

Ronnie stopped instantly, his eyes wide, one of them sporting a bluish ring.

"What happened to your face Ronnie?"

"Nothing," Uncle Ben said, meeting Danny's eyes from the rearview mirror.

Danny looked away, and then at Ronnie, relieved that he had come along. Both were only children in their respective families, and so, were more like brothers than cousins. They shared stories, and food, and secrets that neither would dare tell anyone else – ever. Danny thought Ronnie knew the secret about what was wrong with his father, so he asked, his voice a whisper.

"He got sick at work. *Shhh*, my father's tellin' your mother the story now."

The boys leaned forward trying to follow the conversation. The adults were talking too fast for Danny to hear the details though, and the *chug, chug, chug* of the engine didn't help. Uncle Ben handed Miriam a handkerchief, which she used to dab at her eyes. Danny had never seen his mother cry before.

"I'm real scared, Ronnie," Danny whispered, but Ronnie did not reply.

When they arrived at Boston State Hospital Miriam started to stammer. "What....what happens if our... our medical, um, insurance doesn't pay for Jeff's treatment? How will I get here? I... I don't know how to drive. How will –

"There ain't nothin' to worry about Miriam," Uncle Ben soothed. "I'll drive you around and stuff. Take ya shoppin' and... doan worry." He shut off the engine. "Ronnie, help your aunt out of the car."

Boston State Hospital was a mass of imposing red brick buildings. Inside the reception area, Danny was assaulted with the smell of harsh chemicals, like the ones his mother used when she did her spring cleaning. There was a man lying on a stretcher nearby, moaning; the top of his head wrapped in a white bandage.

"He looks like a mummy," Ronnie giggled, and Danny said, "Aren't mummy's *dead*?" and wondered if his father was going to die.

The foursome strode up to a long desk, and Uncle Ben spoke to a woman standing behind it. Danny noticed the little white hat pinned to her head. He thought she would look prettier without it because then everyone could see all of her nice blonde hair.

"We're here to see Jeffery Oxman," Uncle Ben stated, drumming his fingertips on the countertop.

The woman shuffled through a stack of papers. "Ah, yes. They

just settled him into Ward A." She glanced behind him. "I'm sorry, but children are not allowed to visit patients."

"Ronnie, you and Danny wait over there a sec," Uncle Ben said pointing to a bench.

They obeyed, but Danny watched over his shoulder at his uncle and the woman in deep conversation.

After a few minutes, Uncle Ben called the boys back over. "Children are not allowed inside the patient ward, but this nice nurse is making, um an…

"Exception," Rose finished.

"Exception?" Ronnie said, and Danny told him, "That means she's gonna let us see my dad. Right Uncle Ben?"

"Right," he replied.

The nurse narrowed her eyes at Uncle Ben, and when she saw Danny watching, smiled over at him, but it was a strange, sad kind of smile, Danny thought.

Ward A where Jeffery Oxman had been admitted was at the end of a semi-lit corridor. At the entrance, Miriam stopped.

"Ben, I'm afraid."

"I know." He turned to the boys and warned, "Danny, your papa ain't gonna look the same."

"What do you mean?"

"His face looks different. He can't say anything, but he can hear ya, so talk to 'im just like you would any other day."

Danny shifted his weight onto one leg, wishing he understood what was going on.

Miriam reached for her son's hand, and Danny took it, squeezing it a little, then said what he thought his father would want him to say.

"It's like Uncle Ben told you, mama. It's going to be okay. Don't worry."

"Go on you two," Uncle Ben urged.

They walked inside the huge open ward filled with seemingly endless rows of twin hospital beds lined up side by side. An old woman was asleep in the one closest to the door, snoring. Danny noticed she smelled bad as if she pooped the sheets. Or maybe that was just the smell of the whole place, it was hard to tell. There were nurses tending to patients, and weird glass bottles hanging on poles over some of the beds, and the ward was hot. Several of the patients were calling out, or holding their chests, or groaning. Some of the beds were surrounded by drawn white curtains. Miriam and Danny walked slowly passed them with Miriam counting under her breath.

"Nineteen," she mumbled, and turned sharply to her right, which had them facing one of the closed curtains. Danny felt his heart skip a beat.

His mother sucked in breath, lifted her chin, then pushed passed the curtain with Danny following. Simultaneously, they looked down at a figure lying prone on a narrow bed.

Danny's eyes widened, and he backed off, dropping his mother's hand.

This is the wrong bed, mama!" He gasped. "Papa must be some-place else."

Miriam placed a hand on the stranger's forearm. His right eye fluttered opened.

"Jeff? It's Miriam."

Danny saw that the left side of his father's face was stretched out of shape, droopy, yet stiff. There was a bandage taped to the side of his head, but not all around it, thank God. He didn't look like the mummy man.

He remembered what Uncle Ben had said.

*He can't say anything, but he can hear ya, so talk to 'im just like you would any other day*

"Hi, papa," Danny forced the words out, taking a step closer. "I hope you feel better. You look…um, really good. Do you want to know what I did in school today?" He crept forward, rambling on for the next few minutes while Miriam let her tears flow mumbling, "Oh, my God. What are we going to do? Oh, Jeff! What am *I* going to do?"

# CHAPTER 2

Uncle Ben kept his promise. He drove Miriam to and from Boston State Hospital after he had finished work at the city harbor unloading the catch from fishing vessels, then flaying and weighing the seafood to get it ready for auction. Miriam hated to leave Danny at home in Quincy, even though their modest ranch house was located in a decent suburban neighborhood only twenty minutes from the hospital.

"If you need anything, Mrs. Smithe next door says you can call on her anytime. I'll be home later tonight," Miriam told Danny most evenings before hurrying off.

When neighbors and friends first learned about Jeffery Oxman's condition there was a flurry of activity at the house, with people stopping by with well wishes, and delicious home cooked meals. After two weeks though, the visits slowed down, and then stopped altogether, leaving Danny alone much of every day. He learned how to scrabble eggs; ate bowls of cereal for dinner, sometimes without milk; and found that toast spread with peanut butter satisfied his hunger. Sometimes Mrs. Smithe brought him a home cooked meal which he devoured, but only before he made sure to put some of the food aside for his mother.

On school days, Danny would get himself out of bed and dressed, eat whatever breakfast he could find, then check on Miriam who was usually still asleep, before walking the four blocks to school.

His teachers were sympathetic.

"How is your father getting on, Danny?" Mrs. McGonagal asked one day.

Danny had no idea. No one ever said, except to tell him not to worry. That everything was going to be *okay*, although he sensed nothing would ever be *okay* again.

"I think he's getting better."

"That's good," Mrs. McGonagal cooed. She looked over at Jimmy Patton. "Jimmy? Put that down right now!"

Six weeks later to the day Jeffery Oxman suffered a massive stroke in the insurance office where he worked, he died. He was thirty-three years old.

Uncle Ben broke the news to Danny while Miriam sat like a stone on the sofa absently staring at a spot on the furthest wall. At first, Danny refused to believe him.

"*No, daddy is not dead!*" He screamed. "Daddy is coming home. I just know it. You're *lying.*" He leaped up, beating his tiny fists into Uncle Ben's stomach.

Ben restrained Danny's arms, and Danny felt the pain of his uncle's grip through his grief. When Danny had finally calmed down his uncle told him, "You're the man of the house now Daniel. It's time to grow up. You have to take care of your mother." Then he turned to Miriam, who had not reacted, adding, "She's gonna need all the help she can git."

***

The funeral for Jeffery Oxman was well attended. He had been employed as an accountant for a well-known insurance company, and was well like there.. His boss had closed the office for the day allowing all employees to attend. Jeffery had been a hardworking, loyal employee, and he enjoyed an indisputable reputation. He was also generous to a fault as Miriam found out when Jeff's supervisor sent a co-worker to the house to review the family finances with her.

Mr. Watson arrived at two o'clock one Saturday afternoon just as the leaves were starting to turn color, welcoming the New England fall weather. Mr. Watson wore wire rimmed spectacles, and was dressed in a green checkered suit. He took off his top hat, his face twitching, and with his left hand placed the opening against his chest.

"I'm sorry for your loss, Mrs. Oxman," he said, bowing his head. "Your husband was a good man."

"Thank you. Would you like some tea?" Miriam offered.

"If it wouldn't be too much trouble."

"Not at all." She started to pour water from the kitchen faucet into a kettle when she spotted Danny. "Son? Please go to your room. We have some, um, adult things to talk about."

"Aw, mama. I wanna stay."

"Go," Miriam said firmly.

Danny left the kitchen, but hid behind the couch in the living room within ear shot.

"About your husband's finances," Mr. Watson began clearing his throat.

"Yes?"

Danny heard the clatter of silverware; the shuffling of shoes.

"Jeffery had a small life insurance policy - "

"Oh, that's wonderful," Miriam breathed.

" - And a little savings, but to be honest, not enough to keep you and your son in a strong financial position. He was also generous in making donations to charitable organizations, you see. The *American Red Cross* mostly."

"What does that mean?" Miriam asked.

"It means that you may want to get a job," Mr. Watson said bluntly. "That way you can continue to pay the mortgage on your home when the money runs out."

Miriam had no idea about mortgage payments. She said, "Oh, a job."

She had only worked a short time as a soda fountain clerk in high school. After graduation she had married, and Danny was born a year later. Miriam stayed home to take care of their son. All she ever wanted was to be a good wife, and mother. Getting a job had never been a goal.

"I…I don't have any training. I, what -

"Well, you don't have to get a job *immediately*," Mr. Watson explained. Danny heard paper crinkling. "The good news, Mrs. Oxman -

"Miriam, please."

- is that your husband was a wise investor in the stock market. The worst case, and I do mean *worse case*, is that you will have to sell some of his stock shares."

"Stocks? Oh, um. I don't know anything about that. Jeff took care of all of that," Miriam explained.

"Oh, yes. Of course, of course."

"Would you like sugar?"

"No thank you."

"Cookies? I know I have some -

"No, thank you." Mr. Watson repeated, clearing his throat. "Now, without going into a long explanation, let me just say that you are now sole owner of the stocks and bonds your husband invested in."

"I see," Miriam said, but she didn't see at all.

"If you sell them off, you get cash in exchange for the paper certificates."

Silence, and then Mr. Watson continued. "Depending on how well a company's profits are at the time you sell them…

After a few minutes Mr. Watson fell silent, then said, "I suppose this is a lot of information for you to digest?"

"Well, yes. Actually. It is," Miriam admitted.

The scrape of a chair against the titled floor sounded, and Mr. Watson said, "Well, when and if the time comes that you need to sell some of your husband's, er I mean your shares, I would be more than happy to help you. In honor of your late husband's memory, of course.

Before Danny went to sleep that night, Miriam had come into his room. Sitting on the edge of his bed, she pulled the covers up to his chin.

"What's going to happen to us?" Danny asked.

"Oh, well. I…it's like Uncle Ben, and that nice Mr. Watson said Danny, everything will work out in the end. We have a tough road ahead. I won't lie. It will be a hard road, but we're strong. We can figure things out."

"Yes." Danny agreed, and he thought, *I am the man of the house now.*

"Good night, Danny." Miriam leaned forward, kissing his forehead. He felt her warm lips against his cool skin. Then she reached over and turned off the bedside lamp, bathing the room in darkness.

The next morning Miriam awoke feeling rested. She missed her husband terribly, but she had Danny to think about now. She needed to be strong for their son.

"I'll make you proud of us, Jeff," Miriam said aloud, then went out to the porch to pick up the *Boston Globe* thinking she'd start to look for a job right away – before she really had to – when the headline splashed across the front page caught her eye, which in turn made her catch her breath, and then she threw her free hand across her mouth trying to fully understand the words on the page while sensing the news was not good.

# CHAPTER 3

"We have to sell the house," Miriam told Danny.

"But I don't want to leave!" Danny declared. "Where will we go?"

"I don't know," Miriam admitted. "But we are going to survive. We are Oxmans, and that's what we do. We are strong." There was something in her eyes that made Danny believe her. "Repeat after me," she said, taking both of his hands in hers. "We. Are. Survivors."

"We are survivors," Danny said.

The conversation was taking place just over a year later when *The Great Depression's* lasting effects finally affected Miriam's financial stability. As the economy worsened, and Miriam was unable to find a job, she was forced to go through Jeff's life insurance money faster than she had originally thought. Now she had no other choice but to sell the house. As it turned out, like so many others throughout the country, Miriam was unable to find a buyer. Instead, the bank took it. *Foreclosure* was a word that Danny heard his mother repeat often to Uncle Ben.

"What's going to happen to us now? Danny asked.

"I'm not exactly sure."

"Are we moving to another house in Quincy?" He knew he sounded hopeful.

"No. Some place closer to Boston."

Danny felt his stomach lurch, but he nodded, not wanting to upset his mother.

"Whatever you think best mama is okay with me," he said.

The apartment Miriam could afford was located on the south

side of Boston. It was a cold water, one bedroom flat, with drafty windows, and worn carpeting. The paint on some of the walls was peeling in spots, but it was close to street car rails, so Miriam could at least move around the city to get to soup kitchens and run other errands.

Danny was in shock when he saw the place, but he sensed his mother was unhappy about having to live here too, so he spared her the trouble of complaining.

At Danny's insistence, Miriam moved her meager belongings into the tiny bedroom, while he slept in the living room on the lumpy sofa they had gotten from a thrift store.

"That there sofa is $5.00," the man behind the counter had said.

"Not unless you tell me who died on it first," Danny quipped, his tiny chin jutting out.

"Danny!" Miriam scolded, her hands clenching his shoulders from behind. "Shhhh. Quiet, now," but the clerk only laughed.

"The boy's got a good point, ma'am," he said. "I'm not sure *who* died on it. Go on. Take the darn thing. It's been here forever anyway."

Every night Danny twisted and turned trying to get comfortable, listening to rats scurrying about, and thinking of ways to get him and his mother out of this hellhole.

After the move, Miriam searched endlessly for a job – any job - to no avail. And then a miracle happened, starting with a knock on the Oxman's front door in February of 1931.

A silver-haired man wearing a black wool coat and leather gloves stood in the hallway. His face was clean shaven, and he smelled of expensive cologne. Miriam sensed immediately that he didn't live in the neighborhood, but while she couldn't place him, she knew she had seen him before.

"Mrs. Oxman?"

"Yes?"

"I'm Jim. Jim Jensen."

She stared at him.

"The owner of Jensen Associates."

The insurance company where Jeff had been employed.

And then Miriam remembered she had seen this man at Jeff's funeral.

"May I come in?"

"Oh, of course. Please," Miriam said, opening the door wider.

Mr. Jensen stepped inside. He looked around, frowning. "Nice place," he said, but Danny knew he was lying.

"Would you like some coffee, Mr. Jensen?"

"No thank you. This isn't a social visit. I came to see if you need a job Mrs. Oxman."

Miriam thought she heard him wrong.

"Excuse me? Did you say *job?* I don't know anything about insurance. That was Jeff's -

"Of course, I understand. I know a few families who need their homes taken care of. Windows washed, food prepared. That sort of thing. Would you be interested?"

Miriam's face lit up. "Yes! Oh yes, of course. I'll do anything! Anything at all. I can -

Mr. Jensen held up a hand. "It's nothing. Really. Glad to help. I wish I could do more for you and your son." He looked over at Danny, his eyes lingering on the boy's face. "I owe Jeff so much," he said.

And that's how Miriam started out as a cleaning woman for some of the wealthiest families in Boston, who were lucky enough not to have lost all they had owned in the devastating stock market crash of 1929.

# CHAPTER 4

Danny's new school was fifteen city blocks from the apartment. He didn't mind the walk, except in the cold winter months when New England was blanketed in snow. It was also a tough adjustment living in the city. The people in the tenements around them were not as nice as the neighbors near the Quincy house. He missed Mrs. Smithe and her home cooked meals.

Ronnie and his father came to visit.

"This place sure is, um, well…" Ronnie began and Danny, not wanting him to feel uncomfortable said, "It's awful, isn't it?"

Ronnie nodded. "Yeah. Like my place," he said.

Danny noticed Ronnie had a swollen lip.

"What happened?" Danny asked.

Ronnie turned his face away. "Aw, I just fell at school. It's nothin'."

"Hey, we're goin' now, Ronnie," Uncle Ben called.

"I gotta go," Ronnie said, and turned and hurried away.

***

Danny found his only real pleasure at school. He enjoyed his classes, and his teachers were decent. After the school day ended, however, he dreaded going back home. Although he had tried to make friends when he and his mother had first moved, he soon discovered that was impossible. Most of the other boys on his street were older than Danny; bullies who had lived in the neighborhood their entire lives.

That first summer living in Boston, Danny walked to a nearby park just to get some fresh air. On that hot July afternoon, a thirteen year old boy named Simon Coots, who had sheets of acne along both cheeks, and bulging muscles, sucker punched Danny just for the fun of it. Danny screamed in pain, and surprise. With blood gushing from his nose, Danny tried to fight back, but he was kicked to the asphalt court by Simon and his friends who proceeded to give Danny a vicious beating. Sobbing, Danny begged them to stop while trying to block the blows.

After minutes of lying on the ground in agony, the attack finally ended with laughter, and high five's all around over Danny's head. Simon was the first to turn away, spitting down on Danny.

"Go tell your mommy you got the beatin' you deserved you dirty Jew," he hissed, and then the group went to play basketball without giving Danny another glance.

Miriam Oxman cried when she saw her young son. "What happened?" She asked, wiping blood from Danny's nose.

"I fell in the playground," he lied.

"Oh, Danny! We need to get out of here," Miriam said, holding him close.

"We will, mama. I promise. When I grow up I'll get a good job, make lots of money, and buy you a beautiful home far away from here."

Miriam cried harder against Danny's shoulder.

The next day when Simon and his friends went out to play basketball again, Danny was on the sidelines waiting.

"Hey, man. What's that?" Timothy O'Connor said. He volleyed the orange ball back and forth between his calloused palms, while staring at the opposite end of the court. The other boys followed his gaze.

A rope had been thrown over the rusted hoop. Dangling from the end of it, only a couple of feet above the court, hung Spike. The cat's angled neck was bound in a noose; its limp body swaying lifelessly in a lazy circle. The cat had been a stray that Simon named before telling his friends that Spike was *his* pet, and no one was to go near him unless they got permission from him first.

At the sight of the dead animal, Simon yelped. He cut the rope with his switchblade. Spike's lifeless body fell free. Simon held the cat to his chest, sobbing in front of the other boys. From where he stood a few yards away, Danny laughed, despite the pain. Simon and the other boys looked in Danny's direction.

After that day, Simon and his friends never bothered Danny again.

# CHAPTER 5

Miriam took public transportation to the homes where she worked as a house keeper. She earned enough money to pay her bills, and with some of the generous tips she received, was even able to put a little money away for Danny's future. Miriam knew she was luckier than most people, men mostly, the ones who wandered the streets with cardboard signs hanging around their necks advertising they were available to work. And she – with no work experience at all  was offered a job at the beginning of the worst financial disaster to ever hit the country - thanks to that nice Mr. Jensen, who turned up out of the blue, and turned out to be her best client.

On weekends and during school holidays, Miriam took Danny with her, so as not to leave him alone. She apologized for having to do this, but Danny was glad to get out of the neighborhood anyway.

Danny helped his mother vacuum, dust, wash windows, and polish silverware, reveling in the wealth around him: Crystal chandeliers; round top windows;granite kitchen countertops, and Oriental rugs laid carefully upon oak flooring in rooms that were larger than the Oxman's entire apartment.

As he drank in the opulence, Danny craved this lifestyle, and he vowed to himself that nothing would stop him from getting it.

One day when workmen were unpacking a Teak home office desk from the Philippines, Danny found the invoice while helping to remove the packaging. The price: $800.00 dollars.

"I'm going to buy a desk like this for you when I grow up, mama," he promised.

Miriam ruffled his hair, smiling wanly. "Sure son. Of course you will."

Danny knew she did not believe him, but her doubt only fueled his ambition.

"I will. I'm going to take care of you when I grow up," he insisted. "You'll have more than a Teak desk to brag to your friends about."

"I'll do fine on my own, son," Miriam said. "I just want you to grow up, and be happy with a family of your own."

Danny and Miriam went on like this for a few years. Miriam didn't like that her son had to work so hard, but Danny told her that didn't matter. He was fine. And when he thought about Simon Coots and the other boys, he knew he really was much better off on his own anyway.

When Danny had just celebrated his sixteenth birthday he was helping Miriam at the home of the Jensen family one Friday afternoon when the man of the house came home earlier than expected.

"Oh, I'm sorry," Miram began. "We haven't quite finished. We'll be done –

"That's perfectly fine," Mr. Jensen said. "My family and I are heading to Cape Cod for the weekend."

"I see," Miriam said, just before Mr. Jensen's next words took her by surprise.

"We'd like to take Danny along with us, if you'll have it," he said.

Miriam and Danny looked at each other. Miriam put one arm around her son's shoulders.

"We have a summer cottage in Hyannis," Mr. Jensen explained.

"You… want to take him there for the…the *weekend*?" Miriam tilted her head.

"I think the boy can use a break, don't you, Mrs. Oxman?"

"Well, of course, but –

"But nothing," a voice said from behind her.

Mrs. Jensen walked into the room then. She was home most days caring for the couple's daughter, a fourteen year old girl named Emily, who had dark hair, large eyes, and a noticeable limp. Mrs. Jensen doted on her.

"Don't worry Miriam. Danny will have a good time," Mrs. Jensen assured her. "We want to take him with us. It'll be a mini vacation for Danny *and* Emily. What do you say?"

Miriam looked at Mrs. Jensen, then into Danny's shining eyes, and replied, "I think that's a very generous offer."

Danny spent the weekend at the Jensen's oceanfront cottage, and it was a weekend that changed his life. The beach was steps away from the back porch, and Danny enjoyed walks along the shoreline, and swimming amongst the waves with Emily, and playing volley boy with teenagers from neighboring summer cottages that were a pleasure to be with, unlike Simon and his gang of hoodlums back in Boston.

On the second day there, as Danny and Emily were walking ankle deep in ocean water, Emily suddenly threw her head up, pointing.

"Look Danny, that seagull just dove down for a fish! He's flying away with it! See?" She said, and when Danny looked up, Emily toppled into the shallow water just as a foaming wave crested, covering her body.

Danny scooped Emily up in his strong arms.

"Emmy, you okay?" he said startled.

She spit out salt water while pushing strands of seaweed from her face.

"Stupid leg," she muttere, as Danny gingerly placed her back onto her feet.

"At least you can walk," Danny told her, thinking about his father and how he couldn't walk, or even talk the last time he had visited him at the hospital seemingly a life time ago.

"Yeah, I guess so," Emily moped.

Late Sunday afternoon, as Danny was packing to leave, Mr. Jensen asked to speak with him privately. His wife and Emily were at the beach.

"Sure thing," Danny said.

They went into the den, and sat across from each other.

Mr. Jensen sighed then said, "You're old enough now to understand the story about what happened to your father."

"What story?" Danny asked, and Mr. Jensen told him.

# CHAPTER 6

"It happened years ago…. Mr. Jensen began.

Danny leaned forward in his chair, his heart picking up a notch. "Yes?"

Mr. Jensen looked at Danny, and his words gushed forth.

"The night your father died, he was the only employee working. Long after the others had gone home for the night." Mr. Jensen twirled his gold wedding band with the fingers of his right hand. "I was there too, getting ready for…a meeting with a client. We were scheduled to have drinks to hammer out the details of a contract. Julia and I…Mr. Jensen's voice trailed off, and he looked away for a long moment in silence.

Danny waited, hearing seagulls cawing and rolling thunder outside through the open window.

"Before I could leave for that meeting though, my wife hurried inside with Emily. She needed me to watch our daughter because of a family emergency. Something about her brother. I…I can't remember. Anyway, there was no one to look after Emily last minute, and she was only eight or nine years old, too young to leave at home alone."

Mr. Jensen paused, staring at the wall behind Danny for a moment. Then: "I should have cancelled that meeting. Took Emily home, but I…I didn't. The meeting was too important." Danny heard anguish creep into Mr. Jensen's voice. "Instead, I asked your father if he could keep an eye out on Emmy. He said he would, of course, but he had a few phone calls to make, so I left my daughter in my office, so she wouldn't disturb him. Surely, she would be okay, I thought. I wouldn't be gone long." Mr. Jensen looked at Danny imploringly, and Danny felt the need to nod understandingly.

Mr. Jensen nodded too, adjusting the wire rim of his glasses. "I had left the building, and had walked a block to where my car had been parked, when I remembered I had forgotten my car keys, so I went back to retrieve them, but when I had returned, I saw that Emily was not in my office. At the same time I noticed her absence, I heard a commotion coming from the conference room down the hall. There had been a crew working in there during the day. It's an old building you see, with ten foot high ceilings, and there was a leak up there that needed to be fixed. Anyway, I rushed inside and saw one of the construction workers, a young man with a beard, and your father standing face to face. The workman was holding a hammer, and he swung it at your father's head. Jeff managed to move in such a way though so as not to take the entire blow. And then your father grunted, Daniel – I will never forget that sound; primeval - and body slammed the worker into scaffolding so hard that the structure crashed landing atop Emily. The workman fled. I ripped the scaffolding off my daughter's leg, and that's when I noticed she…she didn't have her blouse on."

Danny's eyes widened.

"At the hospital they said that Emily wasn't hurt, well…except her *leg* had been badly injured. What I'm trying to say Daniel, what I mean, bottom line is, that your father is… that your father saved my daughter's dignity."

Danny felt pride at his papa's heroic deed, but that pride quickly turned to horror when Mr. Jensen's eyes met his and he said, "It was less than a half hour later that your father suffered his stroke."

***

"How was the weekend, Danny?" Miriam asked.

Danny was still reeling from Mr. Jensen's story, but he managed to say, "Great. I swam a lot with Emily, and we had a cookout on the beach one night. I had a lot of fun."

"Good. I'm so glad," Miriam said, smiling. "The Jensen's are such a nice family. If it wasn't for their generosity who knows what would have become of us, Danny. We're very lucky. I will always be grateful to Mr. Jensen."

"Hhmm. Right. Well, I'm going out for a walk," Danny said.

"What?" Miriam turned away from the open refrigerator door. "I was just getting dinner ready. I want to hear all about your trip."

"Later okay?"

"Is something wrong?"

"No. Why would there be?" Danny replied, as Mr. Jensen's last words replayed in his mind.

*The workman was never heard from again. I didn't call the police. I… couldn't. No one knows the real story of how Emily got injured Daniel, including my wife. Please, I beg you to never repeat it.*

"I won't be long," Danny said, and fled not wanting to blurt out what he had learned. The news would devastate his mother, and she had already been through enough in the last few years.

Danny returned at eleven that night when he knew his mother would be asleep, but she heard him come inside. "Danny?"

"Go back to sleep, ma. It's late."

"The trip. I want –

"Shhh…I'll tell you all about it some other time. You have work tomorrow," he said.

When Ronnie and his dad came for a visit the following weekend, Danny told his cousin the story, feeling the burden of the secret lift from his shoulders.

"Wow!" Ronnie said. "That's awful."

"Right?"

"Did ya tell your ma?"

"No, Ronnie. Mr. Jensen begged me not to tell anyone, so please don't say anything either! Not a word."

"Nah. Why would I?" Ronnie said. "Wanna play some hoop?"

# CHAPTER 7

At the end of his senior year in high school Miriam begged Danny to start applying for a secure job in the textile manufacturing mills in Lowell Massachusetts, but Danny adamantly refused. He had bigger plans.

"I'm going to college," he told her.

"What?" Miriam's eyes widened. "That's a grand idea son, but we can't afford to send you to college. I mean, *how* -

"Don't worry." Danny held up a sheet of paper, grinning. "I've already been accepted to Boston State University. I plan to study medicine."

Miriam took the letter and slipped on reading glasses, her eyes scanning the words on the page. "This is great, son. A fine *future* goal," Miriam began, hoping she sounded encouraging, "but we can't afford -

"I took out student loans –

"You did *what*?"

" – and lined up two part-time jobs, which will help me pay for tuition. It's going to be fine."

Miriam shook her head. "When did you decide to become a doctor?"

It was a good question. In the recesses of his mind Danny vaguely remembered the man from his father's office tell his mother that her husband was... *generous in making donations to charitable organizations. The American Red Cross...*and then an image of the mummy man, and his father lying helpless in a hospital bed.

"Years ago. It's like I've been saying all along, ma. I'm going to take care of you until the day you die."

Miriam smiled thinly, secretly pleased that Danny was so determined to care for her in her old age, which was fast approaching she thought.

"And I've been telling *you* son. I'll do fine on my own." Haven't we done so this far? I mean –

Danny held up a hand. "I've made up my mind," he said.

Miriam sighed, studying her son's eager face. The older Danny got, the more he reminded her of Jeff.

"Well, if you really think you can –

"I *know* I can," Danny said, tilting his chin upwards, reminding Miriam of the day he convinced the thrift store clerk to give them a free sofa.

"Wait right here, Danny."

Miriam disappeared, then returned, holding a small blue covered booklet.

"What's that?"

"I managed to put aside some of my tip money for you over the years," she explained, handing him the bank book.

Danny looked at the last page: $1,512.62.

*A fortune!*

"Mama, I *can't* –

"Yes you can. It's for you son. Everything I've done has always been for you," she said, folding his fingers around the cardboard square.

"But what about –

"I never really thought you'd do well in textile work, anyway," Miriam sighed. "You have too much spunk in you."

***

A slight hearing impairment at birth kept Danny out of the draft during World War II, so he was afforded the luxury of pursuing higher education. Ronnie was not so lucky. He was drafted into the army; sent overseas. Saddened by his cousin's departure, Danny saw Ronnie off at Otis Army Airfield in Falmouth, hoping for his safe return. Just before Ronnie boarded the plane, Danny observed his cousin was too thin, his face drawn. He worried how Ronnie would fare in Germany.

"I'll pray for you," he told him.

"I'll need more than a prayer, Danny," Ronnie said, then he patted down his camouflage shirt adding, "Hey, maybe when I get back all the ladies will be after me. Doan women love men in uniform?"

Danny grinned. "They sure do," he said, waving as Ronnie boarded the plane.

That September Danny went off to college. He spent his days studying, and his nights working, pumping gas during the week, and on weekends, as a bartender at a local pub. The hours were grueling; the work physically draining, but Danny didn't care. He knew college life wouldn't be easy. He fell into bed each night exhausted, but his dreams were filled with a brighter future.

Meanwhile, Miriam was working less because she suffered from arthritis in both knees, and that meant Danny had to make up part of her salary, so they could survive. But he managed, and as the years passed, Danny's hard work paid off when he earned his Bachelor of Science Degree in pre-med. Miriam was filled with pride.

"My son the doctor," she teased.

"Not yet, but soon ma," Danny told her. "And then I'll be able to buy you anything you want, just like I promised."

Miriam laughed, repeating as she so often did through the years, "I don't want anything for myself, son. I just want you to be happy."

"I am happy," Danny said. "I have you."

Danny had always dreamed of attending Harvard's School of Medicine for his doctorate degree. He knew it would be expensive, and more work and student loans would be required, but he didn't care.

He filled out the lengthy application, and then waited. And then waited some more for the acceptance letter. He knew his grades were exemplary. There was no way Harvard could turn him down.

"What's wrong, Danny?" Miriam asked when he came back empty-handed from the post office one day. "Did you break up with that nice Linda Saunders?"

Linda had been Danny's steady girlfriend throughout college. She wanted to marry; he did not. He knew that Linda was not the right girl for him.

"No. I'm just anxious to hear from some of the medical schools I applied to, that's all."

He had not told his mother about his plans to attend Harvard. She would have worried about the expense.

Miriam smiled. "What college would refuse you, Danny? You're the smartest young man I know."

"I hope you're right," he said, and Miriam replied, "I am."

When the letter from the Harvard admissions office finally arrived, Miriam was not home. With trembling fingers, Danny opened the seal, gingerly pulling out the sheet of paper buried inside.

*Dear Mr. Oxman,*

*After reviewing your transcripts…rather impressive…we are sorry to inform you –*

The rejection letter was like a slap in the face. Danny agonized over every word, then tore the paper to shreds, convincing himself it was okay because one day his yet unborn son would attend the Ivy League school.

A few days later, Danny received an acceptance letter from his second choice, a university in Texas that had a decent medical program, and he reasoned, was more affordable than Harvard anyway.

"So far from home," his mother mused. "But if that's what you want, Danny..."

"It's fine, ma. Time will go fast, and then I'll be back and get a good job in a hospital here and be able to support us in a better lifestyle. Don't worry."

Danny was right about one thing. Time zoomed by. After completing his medical studies, and a grueling residency program at a poorly run clinic in Dallas, he returned to Boston after having earned his Doctorate in Surgical Medicine degree, thrilled with his achievements. Now he would get a well-paying job, and finally have the means to buy his mother all the finer things in life. He could not wait for financial freedom.

"So proud," Miriam told him. "I'm so proud of you son."

Danny had gone to his mother's apartment after hitchhiking his way home from Dallas. He arrived unannounced, hoping to surprise her, but as it turned out, he was the one surprised.

"What's *wrong*?" He asked.

Miriam had grown frail since his last visit eight months before, having lost over twenty pounds. Her skin was tinged with a yellowish tint; the whites of her eyes spidery with blood vessels. Alarmed, Danny studied his mother as she tucked his degree into a wooden frame.

"I'm fine," Miriam said. "Come. Let's have tea." She moved into the tiny kitchen.  "I heard from your cousin Ronnie just the other day -

"Cut the crap!" Danny snapped.

Miriam froze. Danny had never spoken to her so harshly.

"I'm sorry," he said, trying to calm down. "But you look *awful*. What is it? What's the *matter*?"

Miriam sat at the kitchen table, her shoulders slumped. "Sit down, Danny."

He took the seat across from her. Miriam reached over the table and took both of his hands in hers. Danny felt panic at the thin, cool strips that were her fingers.

After a moment she said simply, "I have pancreatic cancer."

The diagnosis, he knew, was a death sentence.

"Why didn't you tell me?" He demanded.

"I didn't want to worry you, son."

Armed with his medical knowledge, Danny went in search of the best oncologists in Boston, but his mother had no health insurance, and couldn't pay for treatment.

"Don't worry," he told her. "Everything will work out. You're going to be fine. If I have to find a cure myself, you will beat this disease."

"I know," Miriam said, brushing the hair from Danny's brow like she had done when he was a boy. "I know." Her voice was strong, but Danny saw the doubt in her eyes.

Seven months later Miriam Oxman was dead.

# CHAPTER 8

Bitter, alone, and burdened with debt from his student loans, Danny was hired as an assistant physician at Boston Medical Hospital. The pay wasn't great, but it was only his first job. He worked long hours, and while his career brought him professional satisfaction, Danny was lonely. He longed to get married and start a family of his own. He wanted a son to carry on the Oxman name. What was the use of amassing wealth, he wondered, if not for the pleasure of spending it on the wishes of loved ones? Once that thought entered his mind, Danny went in search of a wife.

It was his cousin Ronnie who had introduced Danny to the woman who Danny would later marry. The men had lost touch after Ronnie had gone overseas during the war, but were reunited at the funeral of Miriam Oxman. They had sporadic phone conversations over the following few months, and then one day Ronnie phoned and invited Danny to lunch.

Danny had missed out on so much of Ronnie's life, so even though he was overloaded with work he agreed.

The men met at the *Red Tower Bar & Grille* along Boston's working waterfront. When Danny saw Ronnie, he was pleasantly surprised at his appearance. The word that came to mind was 'robust.'

They ordered oversized portions of fish and chips served on thick cardboard plates coupled with pints of beer in frosted glass mugs. During the conversation, Danny told Ronnie he wanted to marry, and settle down. After all, he was about to celebrate his thirtieth birthday.

"What happened to that Linda woman your mother had always bragged about?"

"Long gone," Danny said, realizing he had not spoken to Linda in years.

"Well then, I have just the woman for you, cousin."

"Yeah. Who?"

"Rose Kennedy."

"Good one."

Ronnie grinned, signaling their waitress for another round.

"Not Kennedy as in the grand and mighty political family," Ronnie explained, nodding at the waitress when she returned. "Thanks." He placed a $20.00 dollar bill next to his glass. "But her family is just as rich."

"How do you know this Rose person, and better yet, why didn't *you* marry her?" Danny asked.

"Because I got hitched to her sister, Iris."

Forgetting his meal, Danny leaned back, wondering how the hell a poor soul like Ronnie, with no education, or connection among Boston's elite, could possibly marry into money.

"How did you manage that?" He asked.

"We met by chance, and fell in love," Ronnie said shrugging.

"Sounds cliché," Danny said, prodding for more information, but all Ronnie said was, "It's kinda hard to explain."

"Well then, when can I meet Rose?" Danny asked.

"Come on over to our place Saturday night. I'll introduce you then." Ronnie took a long slug of beer, started to wipe his mouth on his shirt sleeve, then stopped, using a bar napkin instead. "But buy a suit first. You look like shit."

When Danny started to protest, Ronnie cut him off. He extracted a crisp one hundred dollar bill from his leather wallet.

"Buy a suit. Rose likes men who are dressed well."

Danny took the money, and the advice, and when he showed up at Ronnie's home a few nights later he was shocked at the grandeur, despite the upscale Wellesley address. A butler met Danny at the door.

"Right this way, sir," he said leading the way through endless rooms of hardwood flooring, antique furniture, chintz drapes, and impressive chandeliers, until they arrived in a great room with a massive cathedral ceiling, soft lighting, and scatterings of expensive rugs in rich blue and brown hues. Instantly, Danny went back in time to when he and his mother cleaned homes like this one.

A fire blazed cheerily in a white marble-framed fireplace. A woman sitting behind a baby grand piano played lively jazz tunes. Two other women, holding delicate flutes of bubbling liquid, were crowded around her *oohing* and *aaahing* when she hit particularly pleasing notes. Danny spotted a bottle of *Cristal* champagne nestled among silver framed photos of nicely dressed people on a nearby side table, including Governor Robert Bradford standing with the prominent basketball player Angelo Bertelli who, if Danny recalled correctly, won the Heisman Trophy, and national title as Notre Dame Quarterback in 1943.

At first, none of the women noticed Danny, but before he could speak, Ronnie walked in from a side door.

"Hey, Danny. Glad you could make it. Dinner is in like, half an hour. Wanna a drink?"

"Of course he would Ronnie," the woman at the piano said. She stood. Danny sized her up, thinking her quite unattractive, hoping she was someone other than Rose. She wore a navy-blue pant suit with a string of pearls, and had short blonde hair with heavy bangs covering a wide forehead. Her facial features were long, and her teeth unusually large, reminding Danny of a horse. Her fingers sparkled with diamond rings.

"Don't be rude, Iris," one of the other women said, shaking her sheaves of brown hair. She stuck out a hand. "Hello. I'm Betty. Iris and I are close friends. Iris here is Ronnie's wife."

Danny accepted her handshake, surprised at the strength of her grip.

"Yep. One big happy family," Iris commented, sipping from her flute.

"Danny Oxman," Danny said.

The third woman stepped forward. Danny studied her, pleased with what he saw. She was beautiful, hauntingly so, with long strands of golden hair, light gray eyes, and soft angular facial features. She wore a floral-patterned dress with an ivory colored ribbon tied at her slim waist, and a shy smile.

"I'm Rose," she said. "Iris's sister."

Danny's breath caught at the sight of her. It was at that moment he knew he had found his wife.

# CHAPTER 9

Danny took Rose Kennedy's delicate hand in his, making a point not to squeeze too hard.

"Nice to meet you," he said.

"Same here."

Iris, watching them, mumbled something unintelligible under her breath, while Betty nudged her, frowning. Ronnie slapped his hands together. "Hey, watchya want to drink cousin? We have everything in this joint.  Scotch, Whiskey. What's your pleasure?" He moved behind a bar with a backlit of mirrored shelving.

"Scotch. Two fingers," Danny said, as he tried to see the resemblance between Iris and Rose. Save for blonde hair, the sisters looked nothing alike.

*Beauty and the Beast*, he concluded.

"Coming right up," Ronnie said.

Iris poured champagne into her half empty flute then downed it while Ronnie poured two shots of *Macallan* scotch for Danny and himself, whistling.

"Iris. I think you've had enough," Betty said, giving an apologetic nod towards Danny. "Sometimes she overdoes."

"Screw it," Iris snapped, pouring more champagne without asking the other women if they wanted refills. The bubbly liquid overflowed, spilling onto glistening hardwood flooring. As if waiting in the wings, a butler surfaced, deftly cleaned up the mess, and silently withdrew.

"Slow down," Betty warned.

"God, it's not like I'm um, ah, gonna drive drunk," Iris snapped.

"Hey, let's get comfortable," Ronnie suggested, handing Danny his glass. "Right this way folks."

The men sat on wing-backed chairs facing the women who were perched on a sofa across from them. Idle chit chat followed with Ronnie eventually segueing into a brutal experience he had endured during the war, his brow wrinkling at the dark memory.

After a few minutes, Iris interrupted. "Enough about all that war crap, Ronnie." She rolled her eyes. "God, how many times do we have to hear those gruesome stories? You were captured by the Germans, and held for what? A month?"

Ronnie bowed his head. "Over a year, Iris," he said, rotating his glass with both hands, watching the dark liquid swirl. "426 day to be exact."

Danny reached over, and squeezed his cousin's shoulder, wondering how Ronnie put up with his wife.

"Yeah. Okay. So you had a tough time. Didn't we all?" Iris snorted. "It's your turn, Donny."

"Danny," he corrected.

"Yeah. Right. So...what's your story?"

"Iris!" Betty scolded. "Don't be so damn rude. I'm sorry, Danny. She's not always like this."

Iris grinned. "Like hell I'm not."

A burning log crackled, startling Rose. A sleek black cat jumped onto Iris's lap, purring. Iris absently stroked its fur, her diamond rings shooting off sparks amidst the firelight. The cat twitched its tail before jumping to the floor.

"I'll see about dinner," Ronnie said, rising abruptly.

"I'll come with you," Rose said, much to Danny's chagrin, although she surprised him by brushing one hand against his arm when she moved passed him, leaning over and murmuring, "Please, excuse us."

Her touch sent an unexpected jolt of pleasure through him. He drank some scotch then, dark and rich-flavored, feeling a warm glow give birth in his stomach.

The moment they were gone an unexplainable energy filled the room. Iris placed her champagne flute on a side table, snuggled closer to Betty, one pant leg riding up her calf. She wore brown loafers with white socks. For no apparent reason, Danny began to sweat. He took another long swig, hoping the liquor would calm his nerves, wondering how to start a conversation with these strange women. Luckily for him there was no need.

Iris eyed Danny, then turned her head, tilted her chin upward, then leaned in, kissing Betty full on the lips. Betty reciprocated. Their soft, pink tongues intermingled playfully as Danny stared, shocked, yet at the same time excited, by this visual display of intimacy.

After a long moment, Iris pulled back, breathing heavily, one hand stroking the silky material near Betty's breasts, before both women turned their heads to appraise Danny.

Betty said, "She's *sooo* good in bed," and Iris purred, "Ditto. Care to join us one night, Donny?"

This time he didn't bother to correct her, but before he could respond a voice sounded from behind him.

"Oh. I see you have met the *real* Iris. My *beautiful* wife. The *love* of my life," Ronnie said, peering into the room, holding one hand over his heart, while Rose hovered behind him. There was no mistaking the sarcasm in his voice.

"And Betty," Rose added, eyes down. "Can't forget her."

The two women remained cuddled on the sofa, Betty stroking the face of her lover, ignoring the intrusion, while Iris played with the pearl buttons of Betty's blouse; the ones resting against her solid waist.

"We asked if our guest wanted to join us," Iris pouted. "But I think he has no desire to play."

Which, at least at that moment, was far from true. The hard-on Danny had while watching Iris and Betty kissing bulged in his crotch. He shifted in his seat, hoping no one would notice.

Then he was saved by the bell – literally - when the butler came in and announced, "Ladies and gentleman. Dinner is ready."

# CHAPTER 10

Danny and the others feasted on Leg of lamb smothered in a buttery sauce and sprinkled with dill; caramelized peas; brown rice; broccoli covered in cheese, and an assortment of breads with flavored jams imported from Ireland.

Iris and Betty sat close together at the long end of the table with Danny directly across from them. Ronnie and Rose sat in the chairs at each end. A silver candelabra surrounded by fresh rose petals made for a lovely centerpiece; the candlelight basking the table in an elegant glow. The food smelled delicious, and it was. The best Danny had ever eaten.

After the main meal, while a maid cleared their dishes, Danny fingered the edge of the table cloth marveling at its intricate detail, thinking he went unobserved, but Iris perked up with, "Old English lace. It was my mother's. Been in the family for generations."

"I see," Danny said clearing his throat.

It was 1949. Conversation turned to politics. Iris spoke favorably about the newly formed North Atlantic Treaty Organization, then about the Federal Republic of Germany officially founding Indonesia.

"Indonesia?" Betty said. "Where's that? The Caribbean? Sounds like a nice vacation spot."

"Asia, darling," Iris corrected, wiping her mouth with a linen napkin, reminding Danny to use his own. "I'll take you there one day, Betty. Just say the word."

"How 'bout a trip to Ecuador?" Ronnie offered. "Now *that's* a place I hear is a tourist hot spot."

News had broken earlier that day that a devastating earthquake had rocked Ecuador, killing thousands of people there.

"Very funny," Iris snorted, giving Betty a long, wet kiss as though to embarrass her husband, but Ronnie seemed unperturbed.

Danny marveled at Ronnie's nonchalant attitude about his wife's shenanigans, not to mention Iris's in-depth knowledge of world events. Confusion of what he was experiencing burned into his brain.

Following desert, which included tea for Rose, coffee for the other, and choices of cheesecake, apple pie, and Neapolitan ice cream, Betty and Iris stood up simultaneously throwing their napkins onto their empty plates. Apparently, this was some kind of a signal, because Ronnie and Rose got up too, even though they weren't finished with their pie. Danny followed, and the group left the dining room.

At the foot of a spiraling staircase Iris swirled around. Taking Betty's hand in hers she said, "Nice to meet you, Donny. We're going up to bed now. Betty and I are simply not night owls, are we darling?"

"No. We like going to bed early," Betty replied, with a sly smile, then winked at Danny.

With a final look at the others, the women ascended the stairs; Iris rubbing the small of Betty's back.

A pregnant pause followed before Ronnie slapped his hands together and asked, "So, cousin. Wanna stay for a nightcap?"

Danny started to decline, but Rose cut in.

"Please do. Don't let those two bother you. Iris is…well, she's a bit of a handful. How would you describe her?" She said, turning towards Ronnie.

"A lesbian bitch?" Ronnie offered.

"Yes." Rose giggled into her hands. "God help us all. There are no other words really. Are there? Iris likes being the center of attention."

"I see," Danny said. The scotch had relaxed him, but not enough to kill his inhibitions. Danny liked being in control better than he enjoyed his liquor. He glanced at his watch. "I don't know about that drink, though. It's getting late and I'm -

"It's not even ten o'clock!" Ronnie argued, rubbing his hands together. "Come on," he waved, moving away. "We need to catch up on our lives, cousin. We haven't really talked much since your mother's funeral for heaven's sake."

Rose pleaded with her eyes. Danny had to admit that he was a bit intrigued with the lot of them; curious to know how Ronnie and Iris hooked up. Besides, he had to admit that he wanted to get to know Rose better.

"Why not?" He finally agreed.

Rose beamed.

In the Great Room the logs in the fireplace burned brightly, apparently having been recently stoked by an unseen hand.

"So, let's get right down to it," Danny said, accepting a glass of blackberry brandy from Ronnie. "Thanks. So ,how the hell did you marry Iris?" He shook his head in bewilderment.

Ronnie smiled, a sad wistful smile, one that Danny remembered from when they were children. Ronnie's expression brought back haunting memories of his own: bullies in his neighborhood, the cat he hung from a basketball hoop, cleaning houses with his mother until they were both drop dead exhausted.

Ronnie shrugged. "As I said. We met at a party and fell in love. Rose?" He handed her a brandy glass.

he sipped, smiled. "Nice." Then to Danny, "It's all quite simple, really. My father wanted Iris to marry. He felt that if she found a man to settle down with the union would spare him any embarrassment, you know, because of the lifestyle Iris obviously wants. She can't help it, you understand. She likes women."

Ronnie piped up with, "Iris tried screwing all the single men her father wanted her to marry, and a few of the chumps actually proposed, but Iris said no to all of 'em. Told her father outright she had no interest in men. Go figure."

Danny weighed his next words carefully. "Don't take this the wrong way Ronnie but… how did Iris wind up with you? You're not exactly in her uh, league."

Ronnie laughed, nodding, sipping brandy. "Yeah, course not." He placed his glass on the bar top. "I was a waiter at that gentleman's club down on Boylston Street. You know, where the rich bastards hang out. When Iris refused to marry, her father came to me and gave me an offer that, how do they say? Is hard to refuse. He asked me to wed his daughter, let her do whatever the hell she wanted in the bedroom, and in return I get to live this kinda lifestyle." He swept an arm around the room. "I also get to screw any women I want as long as I'm…what's the word he used Rose?"

"Discreet. As long as Ronnie is discreet about his affairs, then he is free to do what he wants just like Iris, only I must say my sister and Betty have been exclusive for a while now. See, Danny? This arrangement works out beautifully for both of them."

"What's the catch?" Danny asked.

Ronnie and Rose made eye contact.

"Iris controls the purse strings," Rose said, and Ronnie added, "I have a generous bank account which is often replenished as long as I play the good husband. My father-in-law wants to make sure I never blab to all the society papers about his bitch lovin' daughter and her lover. Bad for business, which is understandable, I suppose. Keeps me in line anyway, because even when I get really pissed at the whore, I manage to keep my mouth shut."

"That's a high price to pay, Ronnie," Danny said, frowning.

Ronnie raised his eyebrows. "For all of this? Nah," He snorted. "What choice did I have anyway, Danny? What? Working as a waiter for the rest of my life making peanuts while living in a cramped one-bedroom apartment in Southie?" He took a long sip of brandy. Danny saw the bitterness etched into his cousin's face, and felt sorry for him. As though reading his mind Ronnie said, "Don't feel bad for me, cousin. I like my life. I like my choices of women."

Danny had no words.

And then Ronnie said something that Danny would never forget.

"I went to fight in the war Danny. The chance to go to college like you was never a reality for me. I guess that's just the way life is sometimes. Oh hell." He shook his head. "Anyone up for another brandy?"

"Who is your father, anyway?" Danny asked Rose, but the question was a formality. He had figured it out when he had first arrived at the mansion.

"Franklin Kennedy."

The textile industry mogul who had bought up foreclosed and abandoned mills, then turned them into profitable clothing manufacturing plants, exporting the goods around the world.

"Nice," Danny said silently vowing to himself that he would help Ronnie escape his sham of a marriage. His cousin deserved more. Danny decided to help Ronnie find a woman he could truly love, while he himself would explore a possible relationship with Rose.

"So, would you like to have lunch sometime?" He asked her now.

"I would love that," she said.

Ronnie studied the two of them for a long moment before pouring himself another drink.

"Cheers," he said, holding up his glass.

# CHAPTER 11

Danny Oxman dated Rose Kennedy for two months, and fell madly in love.

Rose had a sense of humor, she was spontaneous, and an avid conversationalist, although she never talked about current events.

"I leave all that 'what's going on in the world' stressful stuff to Iris," she told Danny.

Instead Rose chatted about her volunteer work; the romance novels she was reading; her house decorating ideas; her travel plans. She had an aura of innocence about her that Danny enjoyed. They had grown up in different worlds. Because of his poverty-stricken childhood, Danny reveled in Rose's naivety about her perception of the world. He thought it one of her best traits.

*Opposites attract.*

In order to satisfy his need for intellectual stimulation though, Danny made it a point to go out with his friends and colleagues to restaurants and clubs. He attended conferences and seminars, played golf, and kept up with the latest medical information published in trade journals. When he and Rose were at home, all Danny cared about was her well-being. Their idle chit chat was pleasant for him; relaxing. They talked long into the night about what they both yearned for: marriage and children.

"A whole house full of them," Rose declared.

"Do you have any desire to work outside the home?" Danny had asked at one point.

"Whatever for? My father is rich, and when my parents die, then

Iris and I inherit their estate. There's no reason for me to work," Rose said, wrinkling her brow.

It was difficult for Danny to understand how people could be satisfied with their lot in life no matter how good. Danny had always wanted more of everything, be it money, happiness, love. There had been too much lack during his childhood for him to feel differently.

"It's nice to date a woman without ambition," Danny told Rose seriously. "I want to take care of you, darling."

Rose laughed. "Good, because I leave ambition to the men in my life. Men like you."

She could not have given him a better compliment.

And so they continued to date.

While Danny had one meaningful relationship in medical school it was a brief affair. The girl had a roaming eye. Eventually, she broke up with Danny, after which Danny decided to pour all his energies into his studies. Except for one night stands in the years before he earned his doctorate degree, he failed to seriously date another woman.

Meanwhile, Danny learned that Rose had dated a variety of men among Boston's elite, starting at the age of sweet sixteen when she came out as a debutante. Although she rarely mentioned them by name, she would vaguely refer to her past when Danny brought it up.

"Were you ever in love, Rose?"

"Love? What is love really?" Rose murmured philosophically.

Danny hugged her, kissing her lips, reveling in the joy he felt at being the lucky man who had snatched her up. "Love is everything," he said, running his fingers through her blonde hair. "But don't change the subject. *Has* there been someone else?"

"Yes," Rose admitted. "But it was a long time ago. It's over."

"Did you want to marry him?" Danny asked, afraid of the answer.

Rose placed both palms against Danny's cheeks, gazing into his eyes. "Marry? No. Not marry," she said, kissing him. "That would have been impossible. You, Dr. Daniel Oxman, is my only true love now."

***

Danny was dying to propose to Rose, but he knew he first had to win over her father, Franklin Kennedy. The man adored both of his daughters. Although Iris had given him a run for his money growing up, his youngest daughter Rose had not; therefore, he was not surprised when a fine young man like Danny Oxman asked for his daughter's hand in marriage. Still, he was cautious.

"I've seen your resume. What do you want to do when you grow up?" He asked.

Danny replied without hesitation. "I want to practice medicine, but ultimately I want to own my own medical research company," he told him eagerly. "I have a dream that one day I will find a cure for pancreatic cancer."

Franklin nodded, aware that Danny's mother had died from the disease. He opened a box on his desk then took out a Cuban cigar. "Care for one?"

"I don't smoke, sir," Danny replied.

But, of course, Franklin already knew this. He knew everything there was to know about Danny Oxman; a team of private investigators had recently finished their background check on him.

Franklin also saw how happy Rose appeared dating this man. Overall, Franklin approved of Danny, liked the idea of him and Rose together. More importantly so did his wife, and so would his inner circle, not to mention the public who adored the Kennedy family prestige.

"My family is Catholic. Would you consider converting?"

Danny thought about Simon Coots calling him a dirty Jew after he had beaten him as a child; his mother turning away from the Synagogue, saying she no longer believed in God after her husband died, and then Ronnie, being held captive and tortured by the Germans during World War II. If there was a God, he wouldn't have allowed any of those things to happen.

"Not a problem," Danny said.

"Good. Very good," Franklin nodded, and then, without skipping a beat said, "You know Daniel, Rose had a suitor once. Someone she was serious about. Young love and all that." He lit his cigar studying the man before him.

"She's mentioned several suitors," Danny said, drumming his fingers on the side of his smooth leather chair.

Franklin nodded puffing streams of blue smoke into the air before tossing his match into an ashtray.

"Love comes and goes, Daniel. So does money. I don't plan on losing my fortune, though. Naturally, you understand that. My daughters enjoy their lifestyles. That will continue with or without you. Neither will ever have to worry about money. I've made certain of that."

"I understand," Danny said, thinking about how he had wanted to do the same for his mother. But Miriam Oxman was dead; Rose Kennedy was very much alive.

"I can take care of your daughter without your money, sir. No matter what happens I will make Rose happy. That's a promise." And even as he uttered the words he thought, *How can you say that? You promised your mother she would beat Pancreatic Cancer...*

"Good," Franklin said, and then he asked almost offhandedly, "Do you plan to have children?"

Danny thought about the son that Rose would give him; the boy who would grow up to attend Harvard one day.

"Absolutely, sir. So does Rose. We want a big family, actually." He thought of what Rose had said and repeated her words. "A whole houseful of children."

"Good, because I can't wait to be a grandfather."

"And I a father," Danny replied.

A brief comfortable silence ensued, then Franklin spoke slowly, enunciating his words.

"You know about Iris, yes?"

Danny considered this question then nodded. "I do, sir."

That's the moment Franklin knew for certain that Rose must be serious about marrying this young man if she told him about her sister. "Well, what do you think?"

Danny looked Franklin in the eye. "I think what Iris does is her business."

Franklin blew a stream of gray smoke into the air above his head. "Iris is married to your cousin. Are you good with that?"

Danny thought about Ronnie and how unhappy he was in his marriage, but he also knew the only way to help him get a divorce, and find someone to truly love him was to impress Franklin Kennedy, so he shrugged and said simply, "My cousin made his bed, sir. Now he has to lie in it."

Franklin's tone suddenly grew cool, his eyes narrowed, and he leaned forward in his chair jabbing the lit end of the cigar towards Danny's face. "If the situation between Iris and Ronald ever comes to light because of you," he warned, "I will have you killed."

Danny leaned back in his chair as Franklin chuckled, placing the stogie in an ashtray. "Not *literally*, naturally, but you would feel the effects. I'm a very powerful man with powerful connections, Daniel. Should you displease me, in any way, rest assured you will never practice medicine again."

Danny had no reason to doubt him. He nodded once, then forged ahead with the words he had memorized.

"Mr. Kennedy. I would appreciate your blessing. I want to marry your daughter, Rose. I promise you she will be happy for the rest of her life. You have my word."

Franklin studied the eager young man before him and sighed. After this talk Franklin felt that yes, Danny Oxman would make a perfect husband for Rose.

"You have my permission," he said.

Danny's heart soared. He started to leave the room when Franklin called out, "Wait, Daniel. There's one more thing."

Danny turned. "Yes sir?"

"Since you love Rose and want what's in her best interest -

"Yes?"

" - you won't mind signing a pre-nuptial agreement will you?

"Absolutely not," Danny said, and meant it.

"Good. I'll have my lawyers draw one up."

# CHAPTER 12

The engagement announcement for Dr. Daniel Oxman and Rose Kennedy made front page headlines around the country. Congratulations poured in. The upcoming wedding in the summer of 1950 gave people everywhere hope of good things to come. Franklin gifted the couple *Hollyberry House* a sprawling mansion located on ten acres of secluded property he and his wife owned in Wellesley, a few miles from where Ronnie and Iris lived.

Rose had been elated when Danny slipped a one carat diamond ring onto the ring finger of her left hand.

"It's beautiful, Danny," Rose said, admiring the precious stone. "I love it. I love *you!*"

The only disagreement Danny and Rose had before the nuptials had been where to honeymoon. Rose wanted to spend six weeks in the Caribbean; Danny a jaunt throughout Europe.

"We can take my father's yacht, sail to St. Maarten, Martinique, Aruba…anywhere we please," Rose said, pouring over colorful travel pamphlets. "The *Merry Mermaid* is a floating hotel. We can dock anywhere we want. Oh, Danny! We'll have so much fun."

Danny was thinking more like England, Ireland, and Austria; he especially dreamed of exploring Germany where Ronnie had been captured and tortured during World War II.

"Europe is rich in history," he argued. "There are museums and art exhibits. We can go to Italy. Visit the Vatican, maybe even meet the pope," he joked.

Rose frowned. "Sounds boring," she said.

Danny felt a pang of annoyance, then decided wherever they honeymooned was no big deal as long as Rose was happy; besides, there would be plenty of other opportunities to travel abroad after they settled into *Hollyberry House.*

It was ultimately decided that they would spend their honeymoon soaking up the sun on the islands in the Southern Caribbean, while sailing aboard *The Merry Mermaid.*

***

The night of their wedding was the first time Danny and Rose made love. Danny knew that Rose was a virgin and as such inexperienced, but he also knew that with time and patience he could make Rose feel more comfortable with sex.

"I'm sorry if I didn't please you, Danny," Rose apologized.

"Shhh. I don't care about that right now. You're my wife, darling. I love you so much," Danny told her.

Rose stared at the ceiling as a cloud passed across the closest window momentarily darkening the room, obscuring her eyes. "I'll try harder next time," she said.

But next time was no different.

"It's okay," Danny assured her. "It's hard to relax the first few times."

Rose nodded, studying her hands. "Yes, Danny. I know."

And the subject had been dropped.

Danny and Rose spent the first two years of their marriage traveling as much as possible, bringing back keepsakes from faraway places. In all that time, Rose had not gotten pregnant.

"Suppose I can't have a baby?" Rose blurted out unexpectedly one day, voicing what Danny had been thinking, but he assured her, "You're fine. Sometimes it takes more time than usual." He took her in her arms, and they kissed.

In the fall of that year, 1952, Rose strode into Danny's study while he was working at home.

"Sorry to interrupt," Rose said. "May I?"

He opened his arms out to her, and she hopped onto his lap. She was as light as a feather. "No problem, darling. What's up?"

"I'm pregnant," Rose said with a grin.

Danny was speechless, then he whooped with joy, the anticipation of fatherhood welling deep inside of him.

"See?" I told you our lovemaking would get better!" He said, kissing her, marveling at how the gods had just given him another one of life's precious gifts. He wished his mother was alive to hear the news.

They bandied about names.

"Mary," Rose said.

"We're having a son," Danny countered. "James."

Rose laughed. "We're having a *girl*, Danny."

Danny thought about his rejection letter from Harvard another lifetime ago.

"No. You're going to give me a son."

Rose opened a book of baby names. "Mary is a fine choice," she said placing a finger against a page. "It says right here that Mary is a Hebrew baby name." She looked up at Danny. "Wished-for child."

"I'm Catholic now," Danny reminded her.

"No, you're not," Rose said wrinkling, her nose. "You go to church with me simply to please my father."

Since she was right Danny laughed aloud and said, "It doesn't matter. Our *son* will be named James."

Rose placed a ten dollar bill into Danny's hand.

"What's this for?"

"A bet. If we have a daughter, I get to pick the name. If it's a son, you do."

They shook on it.

# CHAPTER 13

After a brutal nine months of constant morning sickness, Rose shook Danny awake at four in the morning one spring day in 1953.

"It's time," she moaned.

Danny drove Rose to Boston hospital. Naturally, fathers were not allowed inside the delivery room, but Danny was by Rose's side anyway, because he would have it no other way. He knew it, and the obstetrician and nurses knew it too; none of them would dare go against the wishes of Dr. Daniel Oxman, the son-in-law of one of the richest, and most influential men in the country. They liked their jobs too much.

*"Push. Rose, push!"* Danny urged, squeezing his wife's hand. *"You can do this, darling."*

Rose screamed while sweat formed on her brow, and pushed… then pushed some more until seven long hours later the child was born.

Holding the infant up by its ankles under the harsh fluorescent lighting, Dr. Tomlin beamed, "Congratulations Dr. & Mrs. Oxman. You have a fine son!"

As attendants cleaned up the child, Rose whispered something.

"What did you say?" Danny asked, leaning over her, taking her hand.

"I owe you ten dollars," Rose murmured, and Danny's smile lit up the room.

***

James Franklin Oxman weighed in at a healthy seven pounds,

five ounces. He had an unexpected mop of dark hair, and squinty eyes, and red blotchy skin. He was the most beautiful child Danny had ever seen.

"Watch his head," Rose warned, handing little James over. "That's important. You don't want to injure his neck."

"I think I *know* that," Danny quipped, exasperated, but despite his medical training he felt awkward taking the infant in his arms. As he gingerly cuddled James, he fell asleep in his arms. Danny stared down into his son's face in awe, feeling like the luckiest man alive.

A few days later, after Rose and little James were settled in at *Hollyberry House*, Danny returned to work. As he was drinking a cup of coffee in his office flipping through the newspaper, he spotted the birth announcement in the *Boston Globe*. Seeing his son's name in print filled him with pride.

But something else in the paper caught his attention too. A story about an old childhood enemy: Simon Coots; the boy who had sucker punched Danny in a playground all those years ago.

*Dirty Jew*!

The article reported Simon had been arrested for beating a man nearly to death after a barroom fight. He had been sentenced to serve three years in prison.

"Tough break," Danny said aloud, thinking about Simon's cat, the one he had hung from a basketball hoop after the beating Danny had taken from Simon and his hoodlum buddies.

"Hope you rot in jail, Simon ole boy," Danny snickered, and then he closed the newspaper, and went back to treating his patients.

***

A week after James was born, Ronnie and Iris came to visit.

"How can you stand having a kid around, Rose?" Iris asked, frowning. "Diapers and all that crap. Oh, excuse the pun." She laughed.

"Oh, Iris. Don't be like that. This is your *nephew*, for God's sake.

Here hold him," Rose said, trying to get Iris to take the baby from her.

"God no," Iris said, stepping back as though James had some dreaded disease. "Thanks anyway."

Rose shook her head. "I can't believe you, Iris. You're so prissy." Then she turned towards Ronnie. "How about you?"

Ronnie hesitated, then stepped forward. As Danny watched Rose place their son into his cousin's arms, he could not have been happier. Danny had finally achieved what he had always wanted in life: A beautiful wife, a healthy child, his cousin: *A family of his own.* Even Iris's foul mood wasn't going to ruin this moment.

In a quiet voice Ronnie murmured, "He's a handsome little devil. Congratulations. To both of ya." His eyes got moist. Ronnie handed the infant back to Rose almost instantly though, surprising Danny a little, and then he realized why.

*It must be hard for Ronnie. He's stuck with Iris and he'll never have a child of his own. I must help him,* he thought.

As Danny undressed that night, he gave voice to his concern. "We need to do something to get Ronnie divorced from Iris."

Rose placed James in the cradle beside their bed. "Whatever do you mean?" She asked, tucking the flannel blanket under James's tiny feet.

"I've been thinking that Ronnie should divorce Iris, and find a true love," he said. "He's obviously not happy with his alleged wife and Betty's arrangement."

"God Danny!" Rose said, rubbing moisturizer that smelled like strawberries palm against palm. "Don't even *think* of breaking up their marriage. The two of them are fine. Leave them be."

"Maybe *Iris* is fine," Danny argued. "But I know my cousin is miserable. He was almost crying holding little James today. He wants a son of his own."

Danny threw spare change from his pants pocket onto a dresser, the coins tinkling against the surface.

Rose began to brush her hair with a sterling silver hairbrush, peering at her reflection in a mirror. "My father will kill you. *Please*, Danny. Don't interfere with the arrangement between my sister and Ronnie! Don't start trouble."

"Keep your voice down. You'll wake little James," Danny said, peering over at their son who slept undisturbed in his cradle next to their canopy bed.

Rose slipped under the covers, and Danny joined her. "Let well enough alone," she urged, her voice softer. She propped herself up, and began to rub Danny's chest with long, delicate fingers. "For me. Then she began kissing the skin of his stomach working her way down, down, down...

Danny moaned with pleasure, then intertwined his fingers in Rose's long blonde hair, all thoughts of his cousin and Iris fading fast as waves of pleasure pulsated throughout his body.

*Oh, God!* He thought. *I'm in heaven.*

# CHAPTER 14

Danny spent every spare minute with James. He hurried home from work to play with him, and change his diapers, and give him his bottle at dinner.

"You need to spend more time with me, rather than with our son," Rose complained, watching Danny try to spoon-feed James; trying because James was wiggling his face away. "We don't do anything together anymore."

"I'm tired, Rose. It's always busy at the hospital. You get to see James all day, every day. I don't." James gurgled as if in agreement.

"We need to go out as a couple, Danny. We have a nurse. She can care for James." She saw the look on his face. "Being away from us for a few hours every now and again is not going to scar him for life," she said, placing a hand on one hip.

And so he relented.

The next weekend they went to dinner. During the meal, Rose asked Danny about his day. He gave her cursory answers and finally, unable to stand it any longer, she broke her news.

"I was appointed to the board of the *American Red Cross*," Rose said, with obvious pride. "They chose me over Jane Miller. Can you believe it?"

"That's good. It'll keep you busy," Danny said.

"I'm busy enough with James," Rose laughed, "but I like the people on this board. We're planning a charity banquet for February. I was voted as secretary right off. I can give you the date as soon as I know, so you can put it in your calendar. Of course, I want you there. Jane says -

"Yes. Absolutely," Danny interrupted, glancing at his Rolex. "But now we need to get back home. I want to see James off to bed, and I've got some patient records to review."

Rose frowned. "I haven't finished my tea."

Danny gave her five minutes, and then they were in the car, silently driving home.

***

During the first six months after James had been born, Ronnie, Iris and Betty came to *Hollyberry House* to visit frequently, but after the newness of the baby wore off, only Ronnie stopped by.

One day Danny arrived home early to discover his wife and Ronnie together in the dining room. Rose was sipping mint-scented tea. James, a year old now, was sitting in Ronnie's lap.

"Hey cousin," Danny said, pleased to see him. They shook hands. Danny thought he smelled alcohol on Ronnie's breath at the same instant he remembered his vow to help his cousin get a divorce.

"How's it going?" Danny took James from him. The child screamed, reaching his tiny hands out towards Ronnie, while arching his back away from his father.

"Hey, little guy," Danny soothed, trying to press the stiff child closer to his chest. "It's daddy."

"He's just hungry," Rose said. "Here. Let me have him." She took James, nodded towards Ronnie, and moved away as the men retired to the family room.

"So, how's Iris?" Danny asked casually.

"The same. Still with Betty." He slapped his hands together. "Hey. Can I have a drink, Danny? Scotch will wet my whistle."

Danny hesitated. "Maybe you had enough for today? It's only four o'clock."

"So? You have a job, Danny. I have nothin' to do all day. If I have a few drinks in the afternoon it ain't no big deal."

"Ronnie, you would stop drinking if you divorced Iris. You need to find a wife who loves you, and will give you children of your own," Danny said, clearly frustrated with himself for not having said these words sooner.

"A divorce is out of the question, you know that Danny. Iris and me…we have a pre-nup."

"I can help you with finances. I *will* help you," Danny promised. "I have plenty of my own money now."

"Look. I'll think about it. Okay? Can I have that drink now?" Ronnie said, his eyes darting towards the bar.

# CHAPTER 15

The seasons came and went, summer blended into fall, fall into winter, and so on. Finally, James was about to turn three years old.

"Let's have a party for him," Rose suggested. Danny readily agreed.

"We'll invite everyone we know," he said.

Danny took time off from work, getting involved in every detail. He referred to the upcoming party as 'The Greatest Bash of 1956.'

It was while they were planning the festivities that Danny finally admitted to himself that there was something wrong with James. The child possessed strange physical nuances; things Danny had noticed in passing, but now loomed large in his mind.

"Why do you think James walks like that?"

Rose turned her head. "Like what?'

"Like that." He pointed.

James was heading straight for them, staggering across the yard with his belly stuck out. He fell several times in just as many minutes, and then appeared to have trouble getting back onto his feet. The doctor in Danny emerged. "I don't like this," he said.

"Not to worry," Rose soothed. "I think the cake table should go under the tent in case of rain. What do you think, darling?"

"How long has he been this way? Walking like he is?"

Rose looked over at James, then back at her husband. "Why?"

"Because I want to know."

Rose put a hand to her chin. "Well. For as long as he could walk."

"Which was when exactly?"

"I have it written down in his baby book, but if I remember correctly, I believe he was just over two years old. Don't you recall? We were worried because he was still crawling at that age, but Dr. Stern told us there was nothing to be concerned about. Remember? He said James was just…what were his words? Oh yes, a late bloomer."

"That was then. This is now," Danny said. "Things change."

"You're such a worry wart," Rose said, touching her husband's arm, then moving away to check with the caterers.

From that point on, Danny kept a sharp eye on James. He noted that his son had trouble putting toy blocks together in a particular order; that the muscles in his calves seemed especially large; that he always went down for a nap after strenuous play, and that his speech was not developing in line with his age group.

"Dah, dah."

"James. Call me daddy," Danny said, leaning over so he was at eye level with him. "You're a big boy now. Three years old. Say 'three.'"

"Dah, dah," James said, drooling. His eyes wandered around his bedroom, not focusing on much of anything. Then he began to suck his middle fingers.

"Try again, son. Dad-dy. Call me dad-*dee*."

James started to walk away. Danny pulled his son back gently by his arm, but James fell, smacking his head against the arm of a rocking chair. He screamed bloody murder. Rose flew into the room minutes later.

"What happened?" She demanded, wrapping little James in her arms. "I heard his crying from downstairs!"

"He tripped, but there's no bleeding." Danny replied, examining the child's head. "Not a scratch, just a small bump. No need for concern."

James cried for a solid hour afterwards. No matter how much his parents comforted him, James would have none of it.

"Something is wrong," Danny told Rose when James suddenly fell asleep in her arms.

She started to tell him not to worry, but this time he held up a hand. "Something is *wrong*," he repeated.

They took James to his pediatrician where Danny explained his concerns in detail. Dr. Stern listened, while nodding and taking notes, and when Danny had finished, James underwent a thorough physical examination.

"Well?" Danny said, while Rose was helping James dress.

Dr. Stern had his suspicions, but what he said was, "I'm concerned about your son's enlarged calf muscles, but I want to confer with my colleagues and order some tests before an official diagnosis can be made." He looked into Danny's eyes and what he saw there made him say, "Let's not jump the gun just yet, Daniel. Try not to worry."

The minute the Oxman's left the room, Dr. Stern went back to his office, picked up the phone receiver, and began to dial.

***

Over the next few days, James underwent a series of examinations. A week later the reports filed in seemingly all at once. Dr. Stern sat with specialists to review the test results. The group conferred for only a few minutes before agreeing to a mutual diagnosis.

Dr. Stern made the call. "Danny, this is -

"I know." Every muscle in his body tensed. "What is it? What's wrong with my son?" Danny demanded.

"Not over the phone, Daniel. You and Rose need to come see me right away.

Danny froze. He had trouble breathing. He gripped the headset.

"No. Tell me now. What is it? What is *wrong* with my James?"

# CHAPTER 16

"It's best to review the test results with you and Rose in person," Dr. Stern began. "It is the opinion of the team –

"Now. Tell me *now!*"

Dr. Stern sighed. "There's no easy way to put this, Daniel. James suffers from Duchenne Muscular Dystrophy."

Danny knew about the debilitating muscle disease, of course. In medical school he remembered thinking how awful it would be to have to break this kind of news to parents. Now *he* was that parent. Muscular Dystrophy affected about one in thirty-six hundred males; some during infancy; others later in life.

James was that one male statistic.

"Daniel? Are you there?

A guttural feeling erupted from his throat; raw, primeval.

"I'm so sorry, Danny. We can start treatment immediately," Dr. Stern was saying. "There are many innovative -

But Danny was no longer listening. He knew the treatment would simply keep James comfortable while his muscles rotted away, because there was no cure. His son would eventually need crutches, then a wheelchair, and slowly, painfully, his muscles would continue to deteriorate until finally his respiratory system would be affected, and when that happened…Danny could not bear the thought.

He hung up while Dr. Stern was in mid-sentence, then stared out of his office window, furious about how this tragedy could have befallen him.

That night Danny stopped off at his private club, sitting in a corner alone, drinking scotch. He arrived home much later than usual.

"Danny, are you okay? It's after midnight," Rose said, meeting him at the front door.

Danny stood in the foyer, his brain filled with worry, then broke the news to his wife.

Rose stared at him, wide-eyed.

"My God, Danny! How...how did James get such a dreadful disease? He *looks* so healthy. Maybe the diagnosis is wrong."

"We had the best doctors in Boston run every possible test," Danny said. "I have no reason to doubt the results. Besides, the signs were there for quite a while. Let's face it, Rose. We ignored them."

Rose took a sharp intake of breath. "What happens now? She exhaled. "Is he...is he going to be all right?"

"It's a degenerative muscle disease," Danny explained, trying to keep his own panic under control. "A genetic disorder," and as the words burst forth he had a sudden unbidden thought: *Perhaps on the Kennedy side of the family.*

"Is there a *cure*?" Rose asked, one palm pressed to her heart.

"No."

"Is...is our son going to *die*?"

Danny hesitated, choosing his words carefully. "Well, the treatment can -

"He's going to die, isn't he?"

Danny said nothing.

"*Nooooo*!" "Not our little James, Danny," Rose sobbed. "This can't be happening!"

But it was.

In a sudden rush of emotion, Danny embraced his wife. "I'll take care of you both," he said. "I'll do anything to fix this."

"Find a cure, Danny," Rose pleaded. "You're a doctor. *Do* something."

Danny's mind drifted back to the promise he had made to his mother.

*Don't worry. Everything will work out. You're going to be fine. If I have to find a cure myself, you will get well.*

And despite his words, Miriam Oxman had died. Danny had failed his mother, but he would not fail his son.

"I'll do my best," he told her grimly.

The next week he paid a visit to Franklin Kennedy. His father-in-law appeared frail, as though his grandson's diagnosis had aged him twenty years overnight.

"How bad is James?" Franklin asked.

"He could live to see twenty-five, if he's lucky," Danny told him.

Franklin nodded, his blue-veined hands clasped against his stomach. "I heard about that actor Jerry Lewis. He's involved in some telethon for Muscular Dystrophy. I see his poster children on television."

Danny nodded. "Yes. Jerry Lewis is the public relations man behind an aggressive campaign to raise money for research. They're calling the children stricken with the disease, 'Jerry's Kids,' Danny filled in. "From what I understand, there's an outpouring of financial support for intensive research."

"Good luck to them," Franklin said, but there was bitterness in his voice. Something like this was supposed to happen to other people, not to the Kennedy family. He wondered if the disease was in the Oxman genes.

"That's why I've come to see you, Mr. Kennedy."

"Oh? You want to start your own telethon for James?" The older man turned, eying his son-in-law, but Danny was shaking his head.

"I want to establish my own medical research company to experiment with various medications to discover cures for diseases like Muscular Dystrophy."

*And pancreatic cancer*, Danny thought.

"Ah, yes," Franklin said. "I remember you mentioning that desire when you asked me for Rose's hand in marriage. It was one of the reasons I gave you my blessing. Your focused ambition."

"I went over our finances last night, sir," Danny barreled on, excited now. "Rose and I have enough cash to put a hefty amount into purchasing an office complex; however, the combination of the mortgage and personnel costs –

"Say no more. You can have as much money as you need," Franklin said. "I'm getting on in years anyway. I'll be seventy-eight soon." He sighed. "What do I need with all my money?"

"I will make you proud of my progress, sir," Danny said.

"Yes. You most definitely will," Franklin agreed, "by finding a cure for James."

A vision of Miriam Oxman on her death bed loomed large in Danny's mind.

***

While Rose, and an army of nurses, cared for James over the next few years, Danny poured much of his energy into developing Oxman & Sons pharmaceutical Research facility.

"We have only one son," Rose reminded him. "Shouldn't the company be called Oxman & *Son*?"

Danny hugged her close, the words he had been thinking about for months pouring out.

"We can have another child, Rose. Another son. Let's try for one."

Rose sighed. "I'm getting old, Danny. I'll be thirty-four next month. Besides, if what James has is genetic, then it may not be the best idea to have another baby. That's what all the doctors tell us."

"To hell with them. What do doctors know anyway?" Danny said with indignation.

Despite herself, Rose smiled. "*You're* a doctor," she said.

"But a doctor who *knows* he wants another son."

Rose was torn. She contemplated Danny's request, thinking she had not been happy in her marriage of late. Since James had been diagnosed, Danny had been emotionally distant and now so busy establishing his research company they barely spent any time together at all. Maybe if they did have another child Danny would want to be home more. A baby would also give her something to focus her energy on, and James would have a sibling to play with. Still she was hesitant.

"I don't know, What if we have another baby with Muscular Dystrophy? What then?"

"There's only a twenty-five percent chance that'll happen, which leaves a seventy five percent chance it won't; therefore, having another child is a calculated risk worth taking, don't you agree?" Danny argued.

Rose peered over at James propped up in a wheel chair, his right arm draped across a side handle, palm up. A bit of drool hung off his chin. He was six years old now.

"I'm scared," she whispered.

"Me too," Danny said. "However, being scared is not a reason to stop living."

In the end they decided to go for it.

# CHAPTER 17

A year later, Rose cautiously announced, "I'm pregnant."

They were quietly optimistic.

"You're going to give me another son," Danny told her earnestly, but this time Rose didn't bother with her ten dollar bet for names. Instead, she went to church and prayed for a healthy baby.

Seven months later her wish came true. Following a five-hour labor in the early morning hours of March 27th, 1961, Mary Iris Oxman came into the world.

"I'm sorry," Rose said, cradling the infant. "I feel like I let you down, Danny. I know how much you wanted a son."

"Don't be," Danny said, trying to keep the disappointment out of his voice.

Over the next several years as James's disease ravished his body, Mary's health flourished. From birth she showed extensive developmental progress. She sat up without assistance at six months old, and began walking before her first birthday. James adored his sister, reaching out his hands for her, smiling, forever wanting to play.

"Sist-ah," he said, and Danny constantly corrected him. "Sister. Say sist-*er*, James."

But James only repeated, "Sist-ha," while drool dribbled down his chin.

By the time she was two years old, Mary was talking in full sentences using an extensive vocabulary.

"She's pretty smart for a girl," Danny remarked, and Rose lifted her eyebrows at him.

"For a *girl*?" She said, and Danny thought about how much smarter Mary would sound if she had been born a boy.

"For a girl," he repeated, wiping drool from his son's lips.

***

Over the next several years, Rose kept busy raising the children, especially tending to the special needs of James. She slowed down in her volunteer duties too, choosing to stay home more, despite the pressure of caring for both children, which proved exhausting even with help of nannies. While she had hoped Danny would spend more time with them after Mary was born, that was not the case. Rose felt guilty about that too, because she was certain if she had given birth to a son Danny would want to be home more often.

Meanwhile, Danny poured much of his energy into expanding Oxman & Sons, Inc. He had recently hired two new Yale graduates who were making headway in finding medications to better treat various types of cancers, and now DMD.

Meanwhile, friends of the Oxman's missed going out with them. Rose missed the time she used to enjoy with Danny, and Danny missed nothing. He had one obsessive goal in mind: to find a cure for incurable illnesses. It was his calling in life.

Rose understood Danny's dedication to his career. After all, it was his zest for life, and his ambition she so admired about him when they had first begun dating, but they were not good enough reasons now for them to practically be living separate lives. She tried to talk to Danny about her feelings of abandonment, but he was always too preoccupied to hear her concerns, so instead Rose played a little game. She told herself that time for romantic ventures would come later, after Danny's researchers came up with better medicines for dreaded diseases, and when the children were older, and did not need so much personal attention from her.

Before long it was time for Mary to start kindergarten, and Rose was concerned about how she would handle being away from her brother. Mary adored James. She was six years old, and even at this young age Mary understood and accepted James's limitations. She spent hours fawning over him. Rose worried that it would be difficult for Mary to spend her days at kindergarten without James by her side.

On the morning of the first day of school, Rose heard Mary calling out.

"Mom! I'm ready. Come on."

Rose grabbed her car keys at the same time saw that Mary was hopping from foot to foot at the front door, pigtails flinging about her face.

"Aren't you nervous?" Rose asked, opening the front door.

"Why?" Mary said, and she thought, *I can finally get rid of my dumb brother.*

Mary loathed James, although she dared not let her feelings show. Her parents would be angry if they knew how she *really* felt. The last time she refused to play with him, they took away her dolls for two days! That wasn't going to happen ever again. Not because of stupid James, anyway. He was such a bother, always grabbing at her, mumbling words she had trouble making out. And the drooling! *Disgusting!*

James kept Mary from enjoying play dates with her own friends, and more time with their father when he was home, which wasn't much. It was obvious her parents focused their attention on James, and barely noticed her existence. When James was napping, or the nannies took him to doctors' appointments and the like, was the only time Mary was allowed to play with her own friends, or spend time alone in her room playing with her dolls.

Mary hated that her parents lavished their attention on James. He never got into trouble for anything. They paid their utmost attention to him because he was *sick*, which meant they rarely spent time with her because she was *healthy.*

So, when Rose and Mary arrived at St. Marteen's Academy, an exclusive private elementary school in Boston's Back Bay, Mary immediately let go of her mother's hand, racing off into the classroom. The teacher, Mrs. Stevens remarked, "My, she has a lot of energy, doesn't she?"

"You have no idea!" Rose said, and the women laughed.

"How's James, Mrs. Oxman, if you don't mind my asking? I see his pictures in the newspapers. My husband said he thought he saw your son on TV Sunday night."

"Oh, he might have. James is part of the Muscular Dystrophy Telethon. He's one of Jerry's Kids," Rose offered, craning her neck, pretending to see what Mary was up to.

"How nice," Mrs. Stevens said smiling, but Rose could hear the pity in the other woman's voice.

"Well, I'd better get back to the children," Mrs. Stevens said turning. "Mary? Would you like to say good-bye to your mother?"

When Mary failed to respond, Mrs. Stevens started to ask again, but Rose interrupted. "It's all right. This experience with the other children will be good for her. She's too attached to her brother. She needs a little independence. She'll be fine."

But neither woman realized just how fine.

After her mother had gone, Mary felt a shiver of excitement run up her spine. Finally, she was free! At least while she was at school she would not have to deal with her retarded brother, getting him whatever he wanted, and playing with him for hours. She no longer had to watch him drooling, or help feed him, or be bothered by his constant groping. Every weekday morning Mary eagerly waited for her mother at the front door, anxious to leave.

"You really like kindergarten, don't you, Mary?" Rose said amused.

"Yes, I really do."

"But don't you miss being with James?"

"Oh, mother. More than you know," Mary gushed. "But Dad says going to school is really important. Anyways, I made some nice friends to get my mind off of being without him." She tilted her head, frowning. "I hope that's okay," she added for effect.

"Of course, darling!" Rose said, patting Mary's slender shoulder. "Everyone should have friends." And she thought about her own friends, and made a mental note to make plans to go out to dinner with them with or without Danny.

Mary was proud at how well she managed to hide her real feelings. Proud that she could manipulate her parents into thinking she simply adored her brother. If only they knew! James got away with everything; Mary got away with nothing. It wasn't fair!

"Mary, put away your clothes," her mother demanded.

"But we have maids," Mary retorted. Let them do it," and she thought *James doesn't put away anything.*

"Mary, wash the dishes."

Why? We have a dishwasher!"

*James never put a dish in the sink – ever.*

"Mary, eat with your mouth closed."

"James doesn't," Mary finally blurted out. *That's* not polite either."

"Stop it right now young lady!" Danny snapped. "James can't help what he does. *You* can."

Yes, Mary was sick of hearing things like, "James managed to get out of his wheelchair, and take a few steps today. Isn't that marvelous?" and, "James asked for milk at dinner. Great, huh?" and James this, and James that, and *James, James, James.*

Mary thought something had to be done to correct this obvious wrong.

So, in the winter of 1971, when Mary was ten years old, she started to plan her brother's murder.

# CHAPTER 18

Just after midnight on Christmas morning, Mary slipped out of bed, her heart racing. Other kids might be awake waiting for Santa to shimmy down the chimney, but that was only because they were delusional idiots!

Mary wore a pink cotton nightgown that her mother had bought for her. Pink, *ugh*, but Mary wore it to please her parents, lest they get mad at her for being ungrateful and refuse to buy the pretty porcelain doll she wanted for Christmas. She considered throwing on a robe, but decided the extra material might cause a problem with mobility, so she nixed that idea. Next, she slipped into her sneakers, then went out into the hallway.

First, she checked the master bedroom suite where she saw her parents asleep, her mother snoring lightly. After that, Mary proceeded downstairs through the great room, stopping briefly to admire the seven-foot Christmas tree adorned with colorful ornaments that her parents had collected from the countries they had visited around the world. She stared at the gaily wrapped presents topped with huge red and silver bows; smelling the clean scent of pine. Magnificent! She could almost see the face of the porcelain doll she had asked for.

Then it was off to the servants' quarters just passed the kitchen. She listened: To quiet, save for the hum of kitchen appliances. Mary wanted to make sure the servants were asleep. God, she might give old man Sorenson a heart attack if he woke up and discovered what she was up to. After all these months of planning it would be a disaster if the plug was pulled on her best laid plans at the twelfth hour.

Confident that everyone was asleep, Mary returned to her bedroom. In the far corner near the window she saw James lying on his back in a hospital bed with his mouth open. It was Mary's idea that James sleep in her room.

"He can wait with me for Santa," she explained to her mother. "That would be fun, don't you think?"

Rose was delighted. "What a wonderful idea, darling! I'll have your father arrange for a bed to be put in your room."

Danny was overjoyed when he learned of his daughter's request.

"That's a great plan, Mary. You're always so good to your brother. I think Santa will reward you handsomely for that." He winked at her, thinking about which doll he could add to her collection.

"Oh, I don't need anything special, daddy. I have James," Mary gushed.

Danny beamed.

Now, it was time to celebrate Christmas...on Mary's terms. With her heart slamming, she silently moved to where James lay. As she bent over to take a final look at his ugly face, she accidentally banged into a side rail that clanged, stirring him awake.

"*Wha?*" James mumbled. His gray eyes fluttered open. "Sis-ah," he muttered, his rancid breath causing Mary to recoil. James attempted a smile, his lips wiggling like worms.

"Here James. Let me fluff your pillows," Mary whispered, taking one out from under his scalp.

"San-da? Har ?" He asked starting to drool, which had always disgusted Mary, but not for much longer, she thought. *Thank God!* She frowned, staring down at her poor excuse for a brother.

"Not yet. But soon. Close your eyes, James. Go back to sleep. I'll wake you up when I hear Rudolph come, okay?"

Obediently, James closed his eyes. His breathing was erratic. Mary had overheard her parents recently talking about how his lungs were getting weaker, which was bad news for them; good news for her.

The second James fell back asleep, Mary hopped onto his bed and straddled him. Clutching the pillow, she placed the fabric over his face, and bore down with all her strength, pushing her knees deep into the mattress on both sides of him, the balls of her sneakers pressing hard against the bed covers.

God, for someone with a muscle disease James sure fought hard to get out from under that damn pillow. He was sixteen years old too, bigger than Mary, but fortunately, she was the stronger of the two.

Mary silently gave herself accolades for opting to wear sneakers because they gave her the necessary traction to hold the pillow firmly in place over James's face. She didn't want to think what would have happened if she was barefoot against the satin quilt. Asking her mother for new sneakers was genius too. There would be no dirt marks left behind for anyone to wonder about.

James struggled for what seemed hours until finally he lay morbidly still. Mary kept the pillow securely in place for another few minutes to be certain she had sucked the last breath out of him, then jumped over the railing and onto the floor. The second she did she noticed a horrible odor.

*God, he crapped his PJ's!* Mary realized.

Well, living with that putrid smell all night was a small price to pay for getting the greatest Christmas present of all: A retarded brother out of her life.

Mary wrinkled her nose. She thought about getting the air freshener spray from her bathroom, but decided against it. When her parents discovered James dead in the morning they might wonder where the pleasant scent had come from. No, she would have to live with the stink until then.

Mary rearranged the pillow under James's head, and straightened the disheveled covers, before returning to her own bed, feeling serenely calm. Suddenly exhausted, she fell into a deep, dreamless sleep, that is, until morning, when all hell broke loose.

*"Mary! Mary! Get up! Now!"*

Someone was shaking her arms. She opened her eyes. Her father was staring down at her. "Mary, it's time to get up!"

For a few seconds she had trouble gaining her bearings, and then the memory of what she had done flooded her mind.

"Did Santa come?" She asked, her heart rate picking up.

"Yes. That's it. Santa came. Go downstairs with your uncle now, Mary. Go on!"

Ronnie appeared. "C'mon Mary. We'll go see the presents. K?"

Mary got out of bed, taking Ronnie's proffered hand. "What smells so bad?" She asked. She started to turn her head towards James's bed, but Ronnie pulled her away in the opposite direction.

"You're brother had a…sorta accident during the night," he responded. "No big deal."

Mary allowed herself to be led out of the room, but not before she managed to turn and see her mother sobbing into her hands, while her father was expertly examining James's body.

*I did it!* Mary thought with jubilation.

Aunt Iris was in the great room with her friend Betty. Mary didn't know much about Betty, but she liked her a lot. Aunt Iris too. They were fun, not all stuffy like her parents.

Mary beamed at the presents piled under the Christmas tree, her eyes shining in anticipation.

"Can I open some now?" She asked.

"You need to wait," Aunt Iris told her lighting a cigarette. She pulled smoke into her lungs, immediately letting out a little cough. The gesture reminded Mary of how James was unable to breath under the pressure of the pillow.

"Why?"

Betty shifted in her chair. "Well, it's because…" she swallowed, unable to go on. She looked helplessly at Mary, then at Iris, then Ronnie, then back at Mary, then at the ceiling, then started to cry.

"Your brother is dead," Iris said bluntly. "I'm sorry."

But Mary wasn't sorry at all. She was elated at her success! She managed to drum up a few tears though, blinking rapidly so they were forced to spill over onto her cheeks.

Betty started to moan. "*Poooor* James," while Mary forced herself not to roll her eyes.

Ronnie left the room, then came back holding a glass in one hand. Mary was unsure which type of alcohol her uncle drank, but the smell of it was familiar yet stronger now.

After what seemed an eternity, Danny appeared, his face deathly white. He sat on a plush chair staring at the tree in silence, a sudden tension evident in the air. No words were spoken for several agonizing minutes, then Danny said, "Mary?"

She went over to him. "Aunt Iris told me about James. Is he *really* dead?" She felt one tear roll down her cheek.

"Yes, darling," Danny said dully. "He…unfortunately, he suffocated in his sleep. His lungs were bad. You know that. I'm sorry, but the presents will have to wait."

*Shit*, Mary thought managing not to show her disappointment, but happy in the knowledge that this was the last time James would have a negative impact on her life.

Ever.

# CHAPTER 19

Over the next couple of days, the Oxman home was filled with people coming and going, giving their condolences. Mary worried that someone would figure out that she had smothered her own brother to death, but those fears were put to rest when she overheard her father explain to one guest: "Yes. James died from complications associated with Muscular Dystrophy. His lungs were weak. We were expecting...

And Mary had thought elatedly, *I did it. I really got away with murder!*

After the funeral, Danny went into autopilot. He came home from work later and later, skipping dinner, saying little to his family. When he was at home, he chose to spend hours reviewing paperwork that he had long since delegated to his secretary, Inga. The only time Danny put his son's death out of his mind was when he was keeping his patients alive.

Meanwhile, Rose sought counseling for her own grief. She also decided to take up cooking on the days the servants were off. Her friends told her it was a relaxing past time, and they were right. On good days, she would pay Danny surprise visits at his office, hoping to have lunch with him, usually to no avail.

"I'm sorry. Dr. Oxman is in a very important meeting," Inga would tell her, looking elsewhere, and Rose would reply, "It's all right Inga, thank you," but during each failed attempt, her heart grew heavier.

Meanwhile, Mary noticed the change in her parents: her father's stoicism, her mother constantly cooking those stupid, tasteless meals, with both ignoring her! She had quite expected that her father would get a clue, and pay attention to her now that James was gone. The reality was not what she had anticipated.

*They are so selfish*, she decided, and tried another approach to gain their attention.

A month after James had died, Mary started an argument with a fellow student in her sixth-grade class for no reason. The argument turned into a physical altercation. Her math teacher had to pull them apart. Mary had punched the other girl in the face, causing a nasty bruise on one cheek, while Mary had walked away with minor scratches.

Following the incident, school administrators decided to sweep the matter under the rug; after all, they reasoned, Mary did lose her brother recently, so they felt her actions were understandable. They managed to pacify the parents of the student Mary had attacked, and they too agreed not to take further action.

Mary began to skip classes. Again, her teachers and the school administration kept this information from the Oxman's. Those poor people had recently lost their only son, why bother them with the fact Mary was missing a few classes? She was an excellent student anyway, and could easily make up the assignments.

When that approached failed, Mary ceased doing homework altogether, and performed poorly on every test in her English and science classes, even though she knew she could have answered every question correctly without even studying. But when she was handed her report card at the end of the term she stared at the grades in disbelief: straight "A's" across the board.

Principal Connors explained to her concerned math teacher, "Dr. Oxman gives generous donations to this academy. It's not a good idea to mention Mary's, um, acting out as it were," he said, and a week later said to her science teacher, "We have allowed Mary to get away with so much for so long now, I don't think it's a good idea –

And so it went.

*Damn it all*, Mary thought, settling back into her old routine of acing her classes, which was easier than trying to manipulate the system.

When Mr. Connors passed Mary's Chemistry classroom on his lunch break one day, he spotted her bent over what appeared to be an exam, writing furiously and sighed with relief.

*I knew she just needed some time*, he thought. *She must be getting used to the idea that her brother is dead. The poor thing.*

If Mary knew what Mr. Connors was thinking at that moment, she would not have hesitated to kill him.

# CHAPTER 20

At the end of eighth grade Mary decided she had everything going for her: Beauty *and* brains. And she was right. She had thick blonde hair, and long lashed blue gray eyes; high cheekbones, and full lips. She was slight in build too, fairylike, which made her appear sweet and vulnerable. She continued to excel in her studies with little effort, and the thought that she got away with murder made her giddy with joy, and proved her superior intellect. Perhaps she inherited the smart gene from her father; God knows her mother was a mindless idiot.

Mary had long since given up trying to gain her parents' attention, and chose friends whose own parents were just as oblivious. She partied on weekends at unsupervised parties where she experimented with alcohol and pot. Danny gave Mary a ten o'clock curfew on weekends, but he and her mother were usually asleep when she came home in the early morning hours. They were so mired in themselves that they even failed to notice alcohol on Mary's breath after some nights of partying.

Meanwhile, Oxman and Sons, Inc. flourished. Money poured into the coffers, and the company's researchers were making great strides in developing medicinal help for cancer patients, but Danny's excitement about the company's success had somewhat diminished. All he thought about now was James, and how unfair life was that his only son died. He found it difficult not to dwell.

On the other hand, Rose, her depression having been lifted to bearable degrees anyway, experienced mixed emotions.

She felt grief intermingled with sadness and loss just like Danny. She had loved James too, but he was dead, and nothing could bring him back. Rose finally came to realize that she had to be strong for Mary, because she knew their daughter was hurting too, even though she rarely, if ever, mentioned James these days. Rose knew that Mary's silence was her way of coping. Since Danny paid little attention to either of them, Rose finally took it upon herself to spend quality time with their daughter to try to ease Mary's unspeakable grief.

One Saturday while Danny was volunteering at The Andrew's Clinic for the poor – a routine he got into at the request of a colleague - Rose took their daughter to an upscale restaurant in downtown Boston.

"It'll be just you and me, honey," she said. "Girl time."

*Oh for the love of God*, Mary thought. *You're a bit late lady*. But she blinked and said, "What a great idea, mom."

After they had been seated, Rose began to reminisce about the past with every topic centered around poor, dear James. Bored, Mary feigned interest in her mother's memories of her darling son, frowning and nodding when appropriate, thankful that she wasn't expected to be tearful after all the time that had passed. When the server appeared, Mary chose the most expensive items on the menu, and began to chow down the moment the food arrived.

*At least she hasn't lost her appetite,* Rose thought watching her daughter eat.

***

During her last year in middle school Mary was named captain of her swim team, and in the spring captain of the softball team. To the delight of her parents, she was also inducted as a member of the chemistry club for gifted students.

"I'm proud of you, Mary," Danny said at a rare family dinner one Sunday. His words surprised her.

"You *are?*"

"Of course, darling," Rose said. "We both are. That shouldn't be a surprise."

But it was.

Mary looked at her father, who was cutting into his steak. She still craved his approval, but she didn't want that to be obvious, so all she said was, "Thank you, dad."

*Maybe one day he'll really notice me without thinking about James*, she thought.

# CHAPTER 21

As Mary spent more time with her school activities and with friends on weekends, and Danny spent most of his time at Oxman & Sons, Inc., Rose found herself alone much of the time at *Hollyberry House.* The empty rooms and the ghost of James haunted Rose, and she felt an unbearable loneliness. She tried to keep busy, but even spending extra time with her volunteer activities did little to ease her sense of isolation. That's why, when Ronnie started dropping by the house unexpectedly, she was grateful for the company.

One afternoon in the late spring of 1974, Ronnie brought Rose a bouquet of daisies.

"To cheer ya up. I picked them myself," he said.

James had loved daisies, smiling and grabbing the soft white petals when Rose would take him out to play in the garden. With tears in her eyes, Rose took a small vase from a kitchen cabinet, standing on tip toes.

"Thank you, Ronnie. That was thoughtful of you," she said.

Rose had her back to him while arranging the flowers. When she turned around, she saw that he was standing a foot away from her looking handsome in a blue cotton shirt and khaki pants. Rose noticed he smelled good too, of cologne, not scotch. She was glad to see he was sober.

"What's going on?" Rose asked as Ronnie hovered close.

"Iris and Betty left this morning for a month-long vacation to Greece or Turkey or somthin'," he said. "Good riddance to 'em."

"Oh, that's…that's wonderful, I guess," Rose said, smiling uneasily, glancing at the wall clock, but it was only one p.m., and neither her husband nor daughter would be home any time soon.

And then Ronnie surprised her by saying, "How do ya think it would 'ave turned out for us if we got hitched like we wanted all those years ago, darlin'? I bet we would be real happy right about now."

"Who can, I mean, um… who can really know for certain, Ronnie?" She stammered. "We…were just kids. My father never would have allowed me and you -"

"*Shhhhh,*" Ronnie whispered, cupping her cheeks with both hands, then bent, and kissed her lips.

A wave of unexpected pleasure ran up Rose's spine.

Instinctively, she leaned in and kissed him back, their tongues intermingling.

In the dark recesses of her mind, Rose went back in time to her carefree younger days when she announced to her father she was in love with Ronnie Oxman.

"He's a waiter in a gentlemen's club for heaven's sake! No, Rose. I forbid you to marry him."

"But I love him, papa!" She argued.

"Love him, fine. Marry him, no," Franklin Kennedy spat, and to make sure there would be no walk down the aisle he had offered Ronnie a proposal he could not refuse.

"Marry my daughter Iris, and live the rest of your life in luxury," he told him. "You will never have to worry about money ever again."

At first, Ronnie had protested, trying to win over Franklin Kennedy, but the textile industry mogul was stubborn as hell. Rose was furious at her father, but when he threatened to cut her off from the family fortune, Rose had meekly backed down. Meanwhile, Ronnie came to realize the futility of his efforts. It didn't take him long to break up with Rose, opting to live a life of luxury with Iris as his wife. Franklin Kennedy's fortune was more tempting to Ronnie than fighting for Rose's hand in marriage.

Now as Rose pressed her lower back against the counter, her brother-in-law pressed his groin against her lower body. She felt his manhood gyrating against her. Pinned, her heart pounding wildly, Rose pulled her neck back whispering, "This cannot happen between us. I'm married…and Ronnie said, "When was the last time you made love to your husband?" And Rose had no answer.

"The servants…" Rose began searching her brother-in-law's eyes.

"What about 'em?"

And Rose heard herself saying, "They have the day off."

Rose took Ronnie's hand, and led him to the master bedroom where they slowly undressed each other. Golden rays of sunlight streamed in through the French doors warming their bodies. Rose undid the buttons of Ronnie's shirt, thinking about the mortal sin they were about to commit.

"This cannot be happening," she murmured, but it was. They began to undress each other, throwing their clothes carelessly aside while kissing, then Rose playfully pushed Ronnie onto his back, so he lay flat on the coverlet. Then she mounted him, allowing his manhood to plunge deep inside of her, moaning with pleasure, "*Ohhhh*, Ronnie," and then it was too late. There was no turning back. Rose Oxman, and Ronnie Oxman went to that magical place before Iris, Betty, Danny, James, and Mary was ever a part of their lives.

# CHAPTER 22

The board meeting went well, better than expected, Danny thought staring out his conference room window, his hands clasped behind his back. Danny's financial team had delivered excellent news: The fiscal house of Oxman & Sons, Inc. was in fine order. Profits were rising into the millions. Even more exciting was that his researchers were close to discovering a new medication that could make Pancreatic Cancer a disease of the past.

*Too late for my mother*, Danny thought, *but good news for others afflicted with the deadly disease.*

And with the assurance that his long-time goals were finally being met, Danny felt gratitude for his good fortune, and with that gratitude a sudden clarity: He was throwing away his family life because of the death of his beloved son. On some logical level, of course, Danny had known the negative shift in his behavior since the day James had died, but he ignored it, too mired in his grief to see others in his family were feeling the same loss. Now, he had a clear understanding of how isolated and selfish he had been; how inattentive to Rose and Mary. Danny stood there for a moment longer thinking before deciding he had a moral obligation to make things right between his wife and himself. Rose, he realized, was not a bad wife, and Mary deserved more of his undivided attention. After all, she had lost her brother whom she too had loved dearly.

Danny picked up a photograph of James from his teak desktop; the one depicting his son propped in a wheelchair with Jerry Lewis holding the handles from behind, both of them smiling directly into the camera. He studied the image for a long moment, carefully replaced it, and then strode out of his office.

"Inga?"

"Yes, sir?"

"I'm taking the rest of the day off. Cancel all of my appointments," Danny told her.

"Are you certain, Dr. Oxman? You have an important meeting with –

"Cancel everything," Danny repeated, hurrying out of the room, his heart light.

On the car ride home, Danny stopped at a florist where he bought a bouquet of brightly colored spring flowers for Rose, thinking how surprised she would be to receive them. He could not remember the last time he had brought home flowers.

On the drive to *Hollyberry House* Danny exceeded the speed limit, anxious to get home. A half hour later he pulled into the circular driveway. He parked the Mercedes outside the front door, then hurried inside.

"Rose?" He called.

The house was quiet, but then he remembered the servants had the day off.

"Rose? Honey?"

Still no answer.

Danny walked into the kitchen where he noticed a bunch of wilted daisies stuck haphazardly in a vase on a counter. Knitting his brow, he proceeded through the house searching for his wife, tapping the foil wrapping of the bouquet lightly against his right leg.

*Where was she*? He wondered. He hadn't checked the garage for her car. Perhaps she had gone out, but then he found her.

And Ronnie.

They were sleeping in *his* bed, curled up in each other's arms; naked.

Rage like nothing Danny had ever experienced before erupted in his stomach, a burning, murderous rage. He knew he could kill. But which one? Ronnie or Rose?

Or both?

Danny hesitated, took one final look at the whore he had married, and the despicable man lying beside her, then he turned, and fled.

The physician's Hippocratic Oath states:

*…If it is given me to save a life, all thanks. But it may also be within my power to take a life; this awesome responsibility must be faced with great humbleness and awareness of my own fragility. Above all, I must not play God.*

Danny drove around aimlessly, and he thought….

*It may also be within my power to take a life…*

Doesn't that one phrase give him license to murder? Ronnie deserved to die more than Rose, did he not? Rose was a mere woman, after all, weak and vulnerable, especially after their son had died. Perhaps she could be forgiven, although not without punishment.

But what right did Ronnie have to bed another man's wife, particularly that of his own cousin?

Danny fumed, blinded by rage and jealousy. And to think he had listened with an open heart to Ronnie's war stories, comforted him when the memories were too much for him to bear! And what about his efforts to convince Ronnie to leave Iris so he could find happiness with a woman who would love him for the good and decent man Danny believed his cousin to be?

How long had Rose been sleeping with Ronnie, anyway? That was a damn good question. The bitch. Maybe this wasn't the first time. Maybe, just maybe, Ronnie and Rose had been secretly running around behind his back, laughing at him while he worked hard to build up the Oxman & Sons, Inc. empire, just like he had promised Franklin Kennedy, so that he could allow

Franklin's daughter and granddaughter to live in the luxury Franklin had always afforded his own family.

Now that Danny thought about it, maybe Rose did deserve to die.

*Above all, I must not play God.*

Like physicians before him, Danny had taken the *Hippocratic Oath*, and he practiced medicine in strict accordance of its covenants, always believing deeply in the oath's inherent meaning: *First do no harm.*

But now…

That was laughable. Danny had no desire to *harm* anyone. Oh no! He wanted to *kill.*

*First, Do Harm*, he thought bitterly.

At sunset, he found himself at the gates of Oakwood Cemetery. He walked along the winding asphalt paths between headstones, listening to the cries of whippoorwills, until he arrived at the gravesites of Miriam and James Oxman. A warm breeze blew. He took with him the bouquet of spring flowers that no longer seemed ripe with color. No matter. He fell to his knees, placed the spray in the middle of the two headstones, bent his head, and wept.

What would his mother want him to do? He wondered, and the answer drifted towards him along the soft breeze at his back: *Bide his time.*

What would James want? He wondered, but there was no answer.

Danny made his decision.

But it would have to wait. There was much planning to do first.

When Danny left the cemetery, he was eerily calm.

Upon returning home, Danny found Rose in the kitchen preparing his favorite meal: Lasagna with meatballs, and garden salad sprinkled with olive oil and vinegar dressing. The kitchen smelled of garlic.

"What got into you?" He said, forcing a light tone.

Rose turned around, a hand to her throat. "Oh, you scared me. I didn't hear you come in."

*I bet!*

"Well, there was no need to expect me home this early, was there?" Danny said.

Rose averted her eyes. "True."

"Is that a problem?"

"Is what a problem?"

"My coming home early?"

"No, of course not darling," Rose said, "Why would you ask such a question?" But Danny saw her hands trembling as she poured the hot meat sauce into a glass bowl.

"Smells really good. You must have been at this all day."

The image of Rose and Ronnie wrapped around each other's naked bodies flashed into his mind. His body tensed, but he was in control of his emotions. Danny prided himself on control.

Rose gave a nervous laugh. "Not really. I cooked the meatballs yesterday. Mary? Time for supper darling," she called.

"Where is she?" Danny asked.

"She just got home from soccer practice."

"Mary? Help set the table," Rose called again, taking potholders out of a drawer. Danny watched his wife, staring into the face of the woman who had wronged him, the woman he had adored, who bore him the son he had longed for, and a fine daughter.

*Bide your time.*

Mary joined them, her hair in a high pony tail. She wore a tight blue striped sundress that accented her athletic body.

"Can't the servants do it?" Mary groaned. "That's what you *pay* them for."

"They have the day off," Rose said, and Danny thought *How convenient*, and Mary thought, *So, that means I have to do this stupid work? God, I hate my mother.*

As the family sat at the dining room table, Rose made strained conversation, Danny spoke when required, and Mary answered her mother's questions about how her day went with one sentence answers. Everyone could feel the tension in the room, but that was nothing new, Mary thought. Not since her stupid brother kicked the bucket, anyway.

"Where are the rolls?" Mary asked. "You forgot the rolls, mother."

"In the corner cabinet with all the other bread, where else?" Rose said, shaking her head, but also realizing that Mary was usually served her meals by the servants. How would she know where everything was kept in the kitchen, or even how to cook for that matter?

"How about we plan to make dinner ourselves once a week? Just you and me, Mary," Rose suggested, wiping her mouth with a linen napkin. "It'll be fun. We can devise our own recipes together."

The idea of cooking nauseated Mary. She forced a smile though, and replied, "Sounds like fun. Any day you want, mom," and she thought wickedly, *Although, whenever that is I plan to be busy.*

After that day, Rose managed to rope Mary into cooking meals once a week, and three times a week, when her husband and daughter were out of the house, Ronnie came by just to chat, and spend some quality time alone with Rose, while Danny plotted...

*Bidding his time.*

# CHAPTER 23

Danny could barely look at Rose after witnessing her naked in bed with Ronnie. The rage he felt at her infidelity festered inside of him. If he had rarely been home before, now he spent even more time away.

"What's wrong?" Rose prodded, but she kept her eyes averted. "You seem more distant than ever."

"I'm busy," Danny said.

*Planning.*

*Plotting.*

*Bidding my time.*

Rose sighed. "Look, Mary has her last soccer game the weekend before Thanksgiving. Can you please plan to be there?"

Danny pretended to study his planner.

"I'm scheduled to work at the Andrew's Clinic," he said.

"That's a volunteer job," Rose countered. "Can't you get someone to cover for you?"

"Poor people need medical care too," Danny quipped, thinking about his mother, and how she had suffered through her cancer woes without proper treatment. "Besides, the clinic is short staffed enough as it is."

Rose said nothing. She was angry at Danny for not spending time with Mary, but she felt guilty as well, for she too avoided their daughter to spend long hours alone with Ronnie. Rose knew she was not in love with him. It was the attention he lavished on her that she craved; sheer loneliness that drove her into his arms, but she also had to admit to being flattered by the change in

Ronnie.

"I stopped drinking because of you, Rose," he had told her. "I want to live a sober life because of *you*."

Rose's heart soared. If she could not please her husband, at least she could make an impact on Ronnie's life. For the first time since her son's death, Rose felt needed.

***

The Wednesday before Thanksgiving, Danny woke earlier than usual. He had twisted and turned in bed, haunted by nightmares.

*But soon I will sleep peacefully again,* he thought rising.

He arrived at the office at precisely seven a.m.

"You're here early, Dr. Oxman," Inga said, looking at him quizzically. "Don't you have hospital rounds?"

"I'd like the phone book."

"The phone book?" She parroted.

"That's right."

"Of course, but I can look up -

"Just give it to me," Danny said, more sternly than he had intended.

Inga nodded, fishing out the thick yellow directory.

Danny took it with him into his office, careful to lock the door behind him. He plopped the directory on the blotter that protected his teak desk; a beautiful custom-made piece which had been imported from the Rain Forest in Central America. Ever since the desk had arrived, he had wished his mother was alive to see it.

Danny flipped through the thin pages, glancing up every now and again as though he was being watched by unseen eyes. Finally, when he spotted the number he searched for, his heart leapt into his throat. He had feared it would be unlisted.

Reaching for the receiver Danny felt his hand shaking.

For a moment, he hesitated, until he remembered the part of the Hippocratic Oath that granted him permission to proceed:

*…It may also be within my power to take a life…*

He dialed. When a voice answered Danny said, "Is this Simon Coots?"

"Nope. He's my dad. Do ya wanna talk to 'im?"

The speaker sounded like a teenager; perhaps Mary's age.

"Please."

Danny heard the receiver drop, clunking on a hard surface while the boy yelled in the background, "Pop! Phone!" And then a woman's voice shouting for someone to take out the garbage.

Rustling and then, "Yeah?"

"Is this Simon Coots?"

"Who the hell is this?"

"Danny Oxman."

Simon was stunned. Why would Danny Oxman be calling him? They had gone in totally opposite directions in life. Simon dug himself deeper into the murky depths of poverty, while Danny managed to fight his way to the top, reaching heights of success that Simon had no idea existed.

"Whatchya want, Danny? I'm a busy man," Simon said, playing it cool.

Danny had rehearsed what he was going to say for weeks, which meant his words slid out of his mouth like butter.

"I want to help you out, my friend."

Cautiously, his mind reeling, Simon ventured, "Help me? Like… how?"

A voice in the background screeched. "*Simon?* Get Chad to take out the Goddamn trash! Right now. What am I? Your ass of a maid?"

"Shut up, Elenar!" Simon snapped. "*Can't you see I'm on the God-damn phone?*

Go on," he said to Danny.

"I want to make a financial donation to your family," Danny told him, gripping the receiver, his knuckles white.

"Yeah, right. What's this about?" Simon asked warily.

If it was one thing Simon learned growing up on the streets of South Boston, it was not to trust anyone. Not even someone he knew since childhood.

"Not on the phone," Danny said. "Let's meet. Down by the waterfront, say sixish?"

*Only rich people said things like sixish*, Simon thought, sensing there was money to be made here.

"How can I be sure this is worth my while?" He said.

"Let me ask you something, Simon. That was your son on the phone just now, yes?" Danny guessed.

"'Tis."

"Then what I have to say is worth your while," Danny replied, and hung up.

At 5:45 p.m., Danny walked along Boston's waterfront watching swarms of fishermen docking their giant boats; throwing anchors overboard; pulling thick ropes and stacking wooden lobster traps while shouting back and forth to each other over the din. They were gearing up to bring freshly caught Quahogs, lobsters, and Cod Fish into the city markets to be sold at auction the next day, a long tiresome trip at sea having ended.

Danny watched the men work with their knit caps, heavy jackets, and bulky boots, smelling the salty air as swarms of seagulls cawed overhead. He stopped to look over the railing, and spotted a dozen jelly fish floating lazily in the cold green water.

At 6:25 p.m., Danny decided that Simon was going to be a no show. Disappointed, he started back down the dock, but then Simon magically appeared. Despite the passage of time, Danny recognized him instantly. As Simon approached, Danny stood stock-still, the hem of his black woolen coat blowing in the breeze, his blue silk tie flat against his starched white shirt held there by a gold stickpin.

Danny noted his age-old enemy was too tall, too thin. He had graying hair, a hint of a beard, and thin lips. Simon looked old. Old, and tired, and hungry, and at the sight of him Danny felt pure joy.

The two men eyed each other.

"Simon," he finally said.

"Danny."

"Come on. I'll buy you a drink."

They went into the *Red Tower Bar & Grille*, the same restaurant where Danny and Ronnie had first reunited after Ronnie had returned home from the war. Danny made sure they sat at the same table, and ordered the same food too - fish and chips with tall glass mugs of frosty beer.

There was no better place than here, he thought, to finalize murder plans.

# CHAPTER 24

"Where are you going?" Rose asked.

Danny stared out the kitchen window watching a flock of wild turkey's in the backyard lurch forward. It was the Saturday before Thanksgiving.

*Yet another major holiday without James*, he thought glumly.

"Don't you remember? I'm volunteering at the Andrews Clinic," he reminded her.

Rose frowned. "Oh, yes. You know you're going to miss Mary's soccer game, right? Her last match. Are you sure there're no one to cover for you?"

"I already told you how short staffed the clinic is on weekends," Danny said, grabbing his white hospital coat. "I made a commitment. Give my apologies to Mary. I'm sure she'll understand."

"Understand what?"

Their daughter stood in the doorway dressed in sweat pants, and a pale green tee-shirt. Her blonde hair hung loosely around her shoulders. She wore diamond stud earrings that Danny had given to her for her twelfth birthday. Holding a soccer ball in both hands, Mary tilted her head.

"I have to work today, honey. Unfortunately, that means I can't make it to your game," Danny explained.

"Okay, no problem," Mary said, secretly pleased. She wanted to smoke a joint with Ellie Carter after the game, and was wondering how she would manage that. Mary knew her father would notice the smell on her breath, and would probably ground her forever.

"See ya later then, dad," she said, walking off.

Rose sighed. "I guess you're right. She does seem to understand."

"Aren't I always?" Danny smirked, turning to leave. Rose stared after him, used to her husband's dismissive manner, but she also wondered if somehow, someway they could find themselves back to each other. Her mind drifted to Ronnie, and how she had abruptly ended their affair two months before.

"I can't do this anymore," she announced. "It's killing me. The guilt. What we had years ago was just young love, Ronnie. We're adults now. We should know better."

Ronnie stared at her in disbelief. Although their affair had lessened her loneliness, what Rose really wanted, what she had a*lways* wanted, was to make things right between her and Danny. It was Danny she loved; Danny she had always loved. If it had not been for James's sickness, and ultimate death, she was sure her marriage would still be intact.

"I'm sorry you married Iris and not me, Ronnie," Rose continued. "Maybe Danny is right. He has always wanted you to divorce Iris, and find someone to truly love you."

"Nah," Ronnie said, slapping his hands together. "I love *you*, Rose. Always have. Besides, Iris and me, we have a pre-nup."

He was like a parrot about that dam pre-nup, Rose thought, grateful that Danny married her for love, and not because of her family fortune, feeling more determined than ever to work on her marriage.

"It's your choice to stay married to Iris, Ronnie. But *we* can no longer see each. Our affair has to end."

A heated exchange ensued, then Ronnie stormed out of *Holly-berry House*, threatening to tell Danny about the affair, but Rose was not concerned. Ronnie was more in love with the money that Franklin Kennedy deposited into his personal bank account far more than he was in love with her. If Ronnie told Franklin Kennedy about their infidelity, he'd be financially cut off forever. Rose knew he would never take that chance.

Naturally, after their affair ended, the two were thrown together by circumstance, mostly at family functions. Rose was cordial to Ronnie, even accepting kisses on the cheek, but afterwards she clearly avoided him. Danny noticed,and understood why. His wife didn't want to make it obvious she was sleeping with his cousin. What better way for Rose to pretend to have no interest in Ronnie than to steer clear of him in public?

*Bide your time*, he thought.

# CHAPTER 25

A soft rain had begun. Danny turned on the windshield wipers at the same instant he ran a stop sign, almost colliding with an on-coming car.

The other driver shot up his middle finger glaring at Danny through his windshield, but Danny only gave an apologetic wave. Nothing was going to spoil this day.

When he arrived at the clinic, he spotted two nurses at the front desk drinking coffee. Danny saw Nurse Tethers first, a young woman fresh out of nursing school.

*God she looks young. Just a few years older than Mary,* Danny thought, feeling a stab of guilt at what was about to unfold, but pushed it aside just as quickly as it surfaced.

The other woman, Nurse McGee, had gray hair and wise eyes. She had been a nurse for twenty-eight years, and had been working on a regular basis with Danny at the clinic.

"Pretty quiet around here, huh?" Danny said, glancing around the empty waiting room.

"Slow for a Saturday," Nurse Tethers agreed, and Nurse McGee remarked that it would probably be hectic later on. "When the men get their bellies full of beer and start their bar fights," she said. "Then we'll be busy stitching them up, and sending them out to do it all over again."

"Well, that's what we're here for," Danny sighed. "To patch patients up."

The phone rang. "It's for you, Dr. Oxman," Nurse Tethers said, holding out the receiver.

"Hello?"

"Danny? Collin here. Just wanted to thank you for the Celtics tickets. Joan and I are heading out now with the kids. You sure you can handle the clinic by yourself?"

"Absolutely," Danny assured him. "No problem."

"All right then. I'll let you know if the Celtics win."

"Sure thing."

For the next two hours Danny sat in the break room trying to concentrate on newspaper articles. Towards early evening when a few patients sought medical help, Danny went from one treatment room to another, in and out, examining one patient, then the next – in and out of every room, always on the move, like a hungry shark.

***

"Where you going?" Iris asked, eying Ronnie. "You look like you just shaved."

"Out."

"With who?"

"Maybe he has a girlfriend," Betty said, half-seriously.

"No such luck," Ronnie shot back, thinking about Rose.

"No, really. I want to know," Iris insisted.

"It's none of your business."

"Screw off then," Iris retorted, not really caring anyway. "Come on Betty. Let's take a walk around the grounds."

"It's raining."

"Then let's take a nap," she suggested.

"Good idea."

Ronnie watched his wife and her lover leave the Great Room, recalling the recent phone conversation he had had with Danny,

"It's been a long while since we got together, just us," Danny said to him. "I want to buy you dinner. We can catch up. I'm working at the Andrews Clinic tomorrow. Meet me there."

"At the *clinic*? It's in er, a bad neighborhood," Ronnie said. "I can meet you at a restaurant down by –

"I won't have much time to eat," Danny explained. "We can just grab a sandwich down the street. At *The Clover*. Our old haunt," he added.

Ronnie wasn't thrilled about the prospect of *The Clover*. "I'd rather meet -

"Are you trying to avoid me?" Danny asked.

"No. Of course not. Why would I?" Ronnie said, wondering if he answered too quickly. "Okay. What time?"

They made arrangements. When Ronnie hung up, he started to tremble, wondering if Danny suspected the affair he had had with Rose. Did she tell him? No, he doubted that. Rose always said she'd never divorce the great Danny Oxman. Did Danny guess? Probably not. He and Rose had been careful not to be seen, even by the servants. Besides, if Danny thought Ronnie had been sleeping with his wife he sure as hell would not be inviting him to dinner now, would he?

Ronnie found himself wandering over to the bar. He hadn't had a drink in over six months. He had wanted to make Rose proud by maintaining his sobriety. Now that no longer matter. He poured himself two fingers of scotch. Picking up the crystal glass in one hand, he studied his reflection in the mirror behind the shelves, looking into eyes he did not recognize.

*Who am I?* He wondered. *What happened to me? I got old before my time.*

The thought was fleeting, though. In the next instant he downed the scotch, feeling the warmth of the liquor flow through his veins. Soon his confidence returned. He grabbed his car keys, and drove over to meet Danny at the Andrews Clinic.

# CHAPTER 26

Nurse McGee rushed into the break room where she found Danny casually reading the newspaper.

"Dr. Oxman! *We need you stat!*"

Danny hurried out into the hallway where he saw Nurse Tethers barreling towards him, pushing a stretcher in front of her on which a man lay. The patient's tan jacket was covered with blood.

"What happened?" Danny demanded, his adrenaline flowing.

"Gunshot to the chest. We gotta Prep him for surgery," Nurse McGee said.

"What in God's name are you thinking woman? Transport this patient to Boston General immediately! We're not equipped to perform surgery here!"

Nurse McGee shook her head. "No time. He has to be stabilized before we can move him."

Danny looked down at the pale face of Ronnie Oxman, as he trotted alongside the stretcher, the fingers of his left hand clasped around the cold steel railing, his gold wedding band clearly visible. At the sight of Danny, Ronnie reached out trying to grasp Danny's arm, but he didn't have the strength. He smelled of scotch, and stammered, "Oh God...I'm, *ohhhh*, I'm *dy-ing.* Help...me...

Ronnie was wheeled into a room that was routinely used to treat trauma patients, although nothing as serious as this.

Nurse Tethers tore at Ronnie's blood-soaked shirt with a pair of shears. Danny saw her hands shaking as she fumbled with the scissors, while he quickly assessed Ronnie's injuries. The bullet had missed Ronnie's heart by nearly three inches; his chest a bloody battlefield.

"You're right, Helen. Prep him for surgery," Danny demanded.

Nurse McGee saw how much blood the patient had lost, and flew into action, gathering up any surgical tools she could find.

Ronnie was beginning to lose consciousness. "What happen'? I beg you Danny…doan let me die…

"You were shot, Ronnie. Don't worry. You're going to be fine." Danny turned abruptly, moving to the sink, and began to scrub up, when he heard Nurse McGee say from behind: "Dr. Oxman?"

"Yes?"

"You *know* this man?"

Danny froze for a fraction of a second. "Yes."

"How well?"

Danny glanced at the wall clock. "He's my cousin."

"*Oh my God!*" Nurse McGee said, efficiently arranging surgical tools on a stainless steel tray. "You can't operate on a *relative.* I'm going to call Dr. Malloy."

"He's not home," Danny said, his voice cool. "I gave him tickets to the Celtics game tonight."

Nurse Tethers threw the remains of Ronnie's shredded shirt into a medical waste bucket declaring, "*Done!*" as Nurse McGee fled the room saying, "I'll check the list of backups then."

When she was gone, the younger nurse turned to Danny, wide-eyed. "What…what do you want…want me to do, now?" She stammered, sweat forming on her brow.

"Everything is going to be alright, Mildred. Don't worry. Help me on with my gloves," Danny directed. "There, that's right."

While Nurse Tethers pulled the latex up over Danny's wrists, he gave her further instructions. "Do you understand what to do?"

"Yes, sir," Nurse Tethers said, before practically running from the room, passing Nurse McGee, who strode up to Danny and announced, "I got in touch with Dr. Cormick. He's on his way over. Twenty minutes tops."

Danny nodded, his eyes expressionless over his surgical mask. "Let's get him under."

Nurse Tethers returned, carefully holding the bag of plasma Danny had ordered.

Before Nurse McGee administered the anesthesia, Danny heard Ronnie whisper, "Hey, cousin, I gotta...gotta tell ya... ya 'bout -

"Not now," Danny soothed. "You'll have plenty of time to tell me what's on your mind later. We're going to put you to sleep now. Okay?"

Then it was lights out for Ronnie.

# CHAPTER 27

Danny had the tip of a scalpel inside Ronnie's chest cavity probing gently to see where the bullet had lodged. Ronnie had lost a lot of blood, and Nurse Tethers was forced to grab another bag of plasma.

Dr. Cormick arrived a short time later, banging through the double doors.

"*Oh thank God*! You made it," Nurse McGee cried.

Within minutes, he was ready to take over.

"Step aside," he told Danny, who hesitated, then placed his scalpel in the tray in surrender, while Nurse McGee handed Dr. Cormick a new set of instruments.

"Ah, good. The bullet missed this man's heart by inches. You did a good job so far. He'll be fine, Danny. I promise."

Thank God," Danny replied, snapping off one of his blood smeared latex gloves, smiling behind his mask.

***

"How could this have happened?" Dr. Cormick roared, pacing inside a cramped clinic office an hour after the surgery. "I don't get it." He turned towards Danny bewildered. "Your brother –

"Cousin," Danny corrected.

"Sorry. Cousin. Your cousin should have gotten through the surgery without a problem, even here. He should be resting comfortably at Boston General right now, not lying stone cold dead in a morgue."

Nurse Tethers was crying inconsolably into a soggy tissue.

"There, there now, Mildred," Nurse McGee said, patting the

young woman's back. "These things can happen in *any* emergency. Don't take this so hard."

"But…but, I may have *done* something –"

"No. You followed instructions, Mildred. This is simply *not* your fault," she repeated. "Not in the least."

As it turned out, Nurse McGee was wrong.

***

When the news hit the airwaves that Ronnie Oxman had died by the hand of an unknown gunman, Simon Coots had just started drinking at the *The Blue Moon,* a crowded, noisy dive in South Boston. Like the other patrons, he studied the television screen, sipping his cold beer, only he did not take part in the buzz of conversation around him.

"My God," a woman said. "Didn't Oxman lose a kid?"

"Yep, and now another relative," her companion said, shaking her head.

"Who the hell cares?" Brayed the bartender, pouring a mug of foaming beer from the tap. "The man thinks he's betta than all of us. And from what I know he grew up right here in Southie like the rest of us."

Simon sat on his bar stool, thinking about the past.

"I don't want you to actually shoot to *kill* my cousin," Danny had told him in a secluded corner table at the *Red Tavern Bar & Grille.* "I'm not talking murder. Just injure him. Shoot him near the heart. Do you think you can manage that?"

"What if I *do* kill him?" Simon whispered, unable to finish his meal. The restaurant was hopping with a noisy dinner crowd the night they met, but they kept their voices low anyway. Simon had to lean over the table to hear Danny's response."

"You won't. And if you do," Danny shrugged. "I'll take it from there. Don't worry."

"What's your price?"

Danny told him.

Simon's eyes widened. He had never had that much money at one time in his entire life.

"Yeah. I'll do it," he agreed without hesitation.

Now, Simon pulled his wallet from his back pocket, placing several bills onto the bar top.

"Billy, drinks for the house all around!" He shouted with a dismissive wave of his hand.

People cheered. Peter O'Malley shouted from across the way, "Where did ya get all that dough, Simon?"

"From an old friend who needed a favor," Simon called, wondering what he was going to do with the rest of his $600.00.

# CHAPTER 28

The funeral, held at a small Synagogue that Ronnie had occasionally frequented, was a private affair, attended only by close family members and friends.

"I'm sorry about your loss, Daniel," Franklin Kennedy sympathized. "I know you had a special relationship with Ronnie."

"Thank you, sir," Danny lowered his eyes. "We *were* close since childhood."

*But not as close as Ronnie was to Rose*, he thought.

Danny let his mind wander as the Rabi droned on, mentally congratulating himself for planning Ronnie's murder to perfection. He thought about the night Ronnie had been wheeled into the Andrews Clinic after Danny knew he had been shot by the hand of Simon Coots.

*The bullet missed this man's heart by inches. He got here just in time. He'll be fine. I promise."*

Dr. Cormick had been partly correct. Ronnie *did* arrive at the clinic in time, but died anyway, as per Danny's well thought out plan.

The coroner's report explained the puzzle. Ronnie had been given the wrong blood type during the transfusions.

"How could you have done such a horrendus thing?" Dr. Cormick snapped at Nurse Tethers before the formal inquest had begun a few weeks later.

The young woman cowered in her seat, her face red, her breathing shallow. She had been practicing just ten months before this tragedy had befallen her, after spending four grueling years in nursing school. She simply could not fathom the disgrace.

*How could I have been so stupid?* She thought.

"I doan...don't...*know*," she stammered, while Danny watched, feeling sorry for her, but someone had to take the blame for Ronnie's death, and it sure as hell wasn't going to be him.

"I told you Mildred that Ronnie was *B* negative," Danny said softly, allowing some sympathy into his voice. "Not *A* negative. I *told* you that."

Nurse Tethers swiped at her eyes with the back of one hand, confused. She was certain that Dr. Oxman had told her the patient's blood type when Nurse McGee had stepped out of the room to summon Dr. Cormick, and it was definitely not A negative. She was sure of it. Jutting her chin out, she said as much now, her attention directed at Dr. Cormick.

"That's not what the order was for!" He argued, slapping his hand with a snap against the edge of a sheaf of papers he held, startling her. "Do you *see*?"

Mildred did. At least, she saw a typed order she knew had not been written up before or during the patient's surgery; they had been understaffed the night Ronnie had been admitted to the clinic, and no one had the opportunity to finish any paperwork until way after the patient had died on the table.

Mildred looked up at all the hostile faces staring back at her; even Nurse McGee looked upset. Mildred's heart sank. She knew she was no match for any of them. Who would believe her word over that of Dr. Oxman, or a nurse who had practiced medicine for nearly three decades? None of these people here, and surely no one presiding over the inquest, which she knew would result in the revocation of her nursing license. Mildred made a drastic mistake, one that cost a man his life, and her career.

Dr. Cormick glanced over at Danny, feeling dreadful. His colleague was a giving, caring man. He did not deserve what happened to his cousin, especially after having lost his son to a terrible illness.

"I'm sorry, Danny. This is such a tragedy."

Danny let out a sigh. "Thank you, Morris," then turning towards Nurse Tethers repeated, "I *told* you, Mildred. B negative."

Nurse Tethers wailed.

***

Danny was deep in thought at Ronnie's funeral, congratulating himself on his success, when Mary approached him. "Dad? It's time to go to the cemetery." She was antsy to get this whole graveside thing over with already. Sally Caster was throwing a party at her summer cottage on the cape, while her parents were vacationing in Italy. Mary had no intention of missing it.

"I can't," Danny replied. "That would be too much for me to bear."

*How dramatic*, Mary thought.

She was ambivalent about her uncle's death; instinctively sensing that Aunt Iris would be happier now that her husband was dead. Mary also saw her mother crying uncontrollably during the service as though her own husband had died. Mary thought everyone in her family was weird, including Aunt Betty, who technically was not a relation, but sort of was…confusing at best. Well, at least James was out of the picture, Mary thought.

***

In the days immediately following the shooting incident, police searched for the perpetrator, but were unable to apprehend a suspect.

"We'll keep looking, Dr. Oxman," Detective Sullivan promised, to which Danny replied, "My cousin was shot in a tough neighborhood, detective. The chances of finding a suspect are nil. I'd rather the department work on cases that have a better chance of being solved."

Detective Sullivan raised his eyebrows, admiring Danny's unselfish attitude. His men were already overburdened, and overtime was difficult to approve. Perhaps the gossip about the doctor's tough exterior was just that – gossip.

"We'll still do what we can, Dr. Oxman."

"I know you will, Sam."

But nothing ever came of the investigation.

***

Rose fell into a paralyzing depression after Ronnie died. She was like a Zombie going through the motions of her days. It wasn't that she had loved Ronnie any longer, it was not that. It was the guilt of the affair that haunted her. She had committed a mortal sin, and there was no way she could admit that wrong. She knew that if she did, there was a good chance she would lose her marriage, so instead she chose to live with the guilt and shame of what she and Ronnie had done.

For his part, Danny secretly enjoyed watching his wife suffer. Ronnie had paid the ultimately price with his life for his betrayal of Danny's trust, and now Rose was being punished by serving her sentence by living in an emotional hell. Even though Danny had gone against the Hippocratic Oath he had taken as a *doctor*, he knew he made the right decision as a *man*. With the hand of Simon Coots, he had righted a terrible injustice that had been bestowed upon him by the whore he had married.

All was well in Danny's world.

# CHAPTER 29

In the spring of 1976, Mary approached her father who was holed up in the den reading a book, and smoking a cigar; a habit he had picked up from his father-in-law. A light knock at the door caught his attention.

"Dad?"

"Mary? Come in, come in," he said, taking off his reading glasses.

At the sight of his daughter, Danny's breath was taken away. With her long blonde hair, and angular features, Mary was the spitting image of Rose, albeit a younger version. It was surreal to watch her walk towards him, and sit in a leather chair across from him, legs crossed.

Mary wrinkled her nose. "You need to quit smoking," she said, waving a hand in the air.

"It's a nasty habit, I know, but don't we all have our vices?" He said.

Mary thought about the joint she wanted to smoke as soon as she was done with her request.

"I suppose so," she admitted.

"So, what's up?"

"Well, I wanted to talk to you about which high school I should attend."

Danny raised his eyebrows. He had assumed she would attend the *Simpson School for Girls*.

"I was thinking *Grayson Academy* would be a good fit," she said, bracing for her father's reaction.

"Mary! Grayson is a *boarding* school."

"I know. But it's only in the Back Bay, not far from home."

"You'll be living in a *dorm* with –

"I know."

"- other girls, using the same *bathroom* –

"I know," Mary repeated. "But I think I would be more academically challenged there, don't you think?"

What she really wanted was to flee *Hollyberry House*; get away from her mother who, when she wasn't roping her into those ridiculous mother-daughter cooking nights, tried to get Mary to talk, and go shopping with her, practically every weekend.

Danny thought about the shit hole apartment he had grown up in, and had trouble understanding why a daughter of his would want to live anywhere else other than this spacious home, but then he thought about Rose and how much his wife would miss Mary living away at fifteen years old, and he heard himself say, "Well, if that's what you want… and Mary, her eyes shining said, "It is. *Oh, dad*! That would be *great*. Do you think it's too late to apply?"

Danny knew the headmaster personally.

"Not at all," he said. "Let's go tell you mother."

"Mary!" Rose said, placing a palm across her chest. "Grayson is a…a *boarding school*."

"We've been all through that," Danny said, squeezing Mary's shoulder. "It will be a terrific learning experience for her. Living on her own will give her more responsibility than she has here." Danny smiled at Mary, whose heart soared. Finally, she was getting her father's approval.

"Well, I don't know – Rose began, and Danny cut her off. "It's all settled. I'll make the arrangements."

Rose knew it was no use to argue. Besides, deep down, she thought perhaps it was the right decision. It wasn't like this house was the happy home she had envisioned after she had gotten married. Since James had died, there was a constant tension in the air. There were times that Rose believed that tension would lift over time. She had also wanted to confess to Danny about her affair, but every time she attempted to broach the subject, Danny steered the conversation in another direction. She wondered if he knew about her and Ronnie, but if that was the case, then surely he would have brought the subject up himself. Danny was not the type of man to hold back his thoughts - or his anger. So, finally, she gave up, figuring she'd simply have to live with the secret, and the shame and guilt that came with it.

*** 

"I can't believe your parents said yes!" Sally Caster squealed, as Mary was moving into their dorm room.

"I know, right? I thought my mother was going to have a heart attack."

"We're gonna have a blast!"

"Yep! We're finally free!" Mary declared, looking around. She had to admit her father had been right. The bedroom was small, and there was a community bathroom down the hall, but that was a small price to pay for freedom.

During her first semester at Grayson, Mary partied hard. Unfortunately, as she was enjoying her wild ways, her grades suffered. During Christmas break her father took her aside.

"I agreed for you to attend Grayson, but I fully expected you to earn better grades, Mary."

Her heart dropped as she watched her dad examine her report card. "What are you doing over there? Surely not studying."

Mary cringed. The last thing she wanted was to disappoint her father.

"My classes are hard," she began.

"Life is hard. Get your grades up or you'll have to move back home, and enroll at Simpson. It's what your Grandfather Kennedy had wanted in the first place. I had to convince him Grayson was the better choice. Now, I'm not so sure."

"Oh, dad! please *no!* I'll study harder. Really, I know I can -

"Do you need a tutor? Your English grades are the worst," Danny asked, frowning.

"No. No," Mary said, then revised her thought. "I mean, if I *do*, I'll let you know."

"One more semester, Mary. One more chance."

"I promise I'll do better," she said.

*But how?*

It did not take her long to formulate a plan.

At the start of the spring semester, Mary approached her English teacher, Mr. Bacardi, after most of the students left the grounds for weekend get-a-ways.

"Yes?" Mr. Bacardi said, looking up from his desk. He was in his mid-thirties, tall and thin, and wore wire-rimmed glasses.

Mary felt a fission of excitement run through her at what was about to unfold.

"I need to speak to you about my grade," she said, moving forward.

"Oh, yes. I'm glad you're taking the initiative," Mr. Bacardi began. "I was starting to worry. Let's see. I have your last assignment, um, right here… somewhere…" he began to shuffle through a stack of papers. "Ah, here it is."

When he looked up again, he saw Mary had taken off her emerald green sweater. She was leaning over the desk, her palms pressing against the surface, her lovely round breasts straining against a low-cut lacy bra. Up close she smelled like wild flowers.

Jim Bacardi felt himself getting aroused. He blushed wildly, then jumped up glancing behind her, grateful that she had closed the door.

"Mary! What on earth are you *doing*? Put your sweater back on,' he ordered, although he couldn't tear his eyes away from her half-naked body.

"I need extra help to improve my class average," Mary purred, her hands unclasping the front hook of her bra. She let the garment fall to the floor, exposing her perky breasts, pink nipples erect.

"I...you must get out of here, Mary! He cried. "We can get into serious trouble for this."

*You mean you can*, she thought wickedly, running her tongue across her lower lip.

"*Please Mary*!" He begged. "Get dressed right this instant!"

Mary's heart rate kicked up a notch, the thrill of getting caught filling her with an arousal that surprised even her.

She stroked the length of his arm, then let out a sigh. "Well, if you insist."

Mary bent over to pick her bra off the tiled floor, knowing full well her skirt had ridden up just passed the rim of her buttocks. She wore no underwear.

Jim Bacardi forced himself to look away, and that's when they heard someone whistling in the hall.

"Oh, my sweet Lord," he murmured.

Mary kicked her bra underneath the desk, and got her sweater back on just as the door swung open. Mr. Watson breezed inside then, pushing the handle of a mop in a yellow wash bucket in front of him.

"'scuse me," he said, backing up. "I was jus' gonna clean this here room. I thought peoples was gone."

"It's okay," Mr. Bacardi breathed. "Miss Oxman *was* just leaving."

Mary and Jim Barcadi left the building separately, but he met her a mile away from school grounds, and then he drove them to a seedy hotel just over the New Hampshire border where neither of them would be recognized. They spent two hours together, and when Jim got home for dinner that night, he brought with him a dozen red roses for his wife, and a fluffy stuffed bear for their toddler daughter.

"Thank you, honey," Louise said. "What's gotten into you?"

Jim thought of what he had gotten into: Mary Oxman, and said, "It was a good day, that's all."

That semester Mary met up with Jim Bacardi every Friday afternoon.

"I'm proud of you, Mary," Danny said at the close of the semester. "You got all your grades up. I see you went from a C to an A in English. Excellent."

"Thanks. I worked really hard, and I love my English teacher," Mary gushed. "I went to Mr. Bacardi every week for tutoring. He was a *huge* help."

# CHAPTER 30

The first time Mary got high on mescaline she was a guest on a yacht that was sailing to Bermuda. It was the end of her junior year at Grayson, just shy of her 17th birthday.

"What is it, Sarah?"

"Nothing that will hurt you," her friend assured her. "It's only a button. Open up."

Sarah placed a round tab onto Mary's tongue. "Now chew," she ordered.

Mary obeyed and soon after she was in heaven in awe of God seated at his almighty throne and she asked him if Jesus was really his son but before he could answer Mary turned and flew through the soft wind that carried her along and through a garden filled with fluorescent purple and yellow flowers that smelled like strawberries and then she was flying on wings tinged with gold with the wind cooling her cheeks and the massive Rain Forest appeared far, far below her and she was laughing as her hair fell about her head tickling her face and then she felt herself tumbling down head over heels landing feet first into a warm clear blue ocean where an octopus enveloped her with such love her heart overflowed with joy and then she felt the slippery sea creature poking a thick tentacle inside her private places sending mounting waves of pleasure throughout her body and then... she opened her eyes to see Tommy Hanson lying on top of her naked body breathing fast, grunting, one palm pressed down onto a mattress, his head turned down to one side, and what he was doing to her was *soooo* much better than Jimmy O'Leary and Ben Zolanta and Timothy Denton and…

"More," she whispered, and Tommy was happy to oblige.

***

Mary's high school years passed quickly. She got to know most of her teachers very well, some better than others, and managed to earn excellent grades in her science classes on her own merit, while still partying her way towards graduation. Mary had a higher than average IQ. She knew this was because James had been born with defects, so God had given Mary a superior brain to compensate for her brother's flaws.

In Mary's senior year at Grayson, Danny approached her, and inquired, "Which colleges are you interested in?"

Mary hadn't thought about college. In truth, she hadn't thought about her future plans at all, but not wanting to disappoint him said, "I…I haven't decided."

Danny thought about his dreams for James, and found himself saying, "What about Harvard?"

"What do you -

"Your grades are excellent. You're a smart young woman," Danny said. "You'll have no problem getting accepted. Would you like to apply?"

His words were like music to her ears.

"Well, I have always wanted to go to medical school, like you," she lied.

Danny beamed. "I had no idea," he said, and Mary thought, *Neither did I.*

"Oh, yes. Pharmaceutical research has been my dream since I was a child."

*Not!*

Suddenly, Danny saw Mary in a different light.

"That's wonderful, darling. When you graduate -

"What's going on?" Rose asked, stepping inside the den.

"I'm applying to Harvard," Mary told her.

Rose looked at Danny, then at their daughter. Harvard had been Danny's dream for James. She had been certain he would want Mary to attend a finishing school, then find a nice man to marry, settle down, and raise children with.

"Are you *serious*?" She asked.

"Why?" Mary placed a hand on one hip. "You don't think I can handle it?"

"I never said...of *course*, I do."

"You don't *sound* like it."

"Why do you –

"*Dad* has faith in me!"

"Yes, I do," Danny agreed.

"See? Why can't *you* have faith in me mother?"

"I *never* said –

"You *insinuated* –

"– *I did not* –

Danny held up a hand. "It's settled. Let's get your application in."

The next morning before her math class, Mary replayed the scene to Sally Caster.

"Harvard? *Seriously*?" Sally said, laughing. "I can't imagine you at that stuffy old man's college. You'll really have to hit the books too. They don't fuck around at that...what do they call it? Ivy league, prissy college."

"Yeah," Mary said, wondering if she had made the right decision.

"Well, if that's your plan, then at least have some fun while you're in prison," Sally suggested. "I hear the boys over there are not only rich, but super cute. That's a plus."

"See? I guess I'll be okay after all. Besides I probably won't have to worry about it. Harvard doesn't accept many women," Mary said.

"Good point. Hey the Zolanta brothers are having a party tonight. Wanna go?”

***

Danny came home early one evening a week before Christmas to see Rose seated on a settee in the living room with the fireplace crackling. She had dimmed the lights, and lit candles that smelled of pine.

“What’s up?” Danny said.

“Mary? *Mary*!” Rose called. “Your father’s home.”

Mary came into the room a few minutes later, holding up a sheet of paper.

“I’m in,” she said, and Danny whooped, giving his daughter a bear hug. Mary hugged him back, scrunching the paper she held at the small of his back.

“Let’s not wrinkle that acceptance letter,” Danny cautioned, pulling back, taking the paper from her hand. “I want to frame it.”

For an instant, he thought he saw James standing in a shadowy far corner, but this James was a grown man, with dark hair and strong arms and legs; handsome in the Oxman way. The vision vanished as fast as it had come though. The past was dead; now the future was all about Mary’s success. It was a bittersweet moment.

“I’m proud of you, Mary,” Danny told her. He thought about the generous donation he had given to the Ivy League school, just after Mary had applied for admission. But despite his influence, Danny believed Mary would excel at her studies. She was, after all, smart for a woman. What Danny didn’t know was that Mary’s brain was getting foggier by the day, due to her illicit drug use.

As it turned out, Sally Caster had been right. Harvard was no picnic. Even though she was an Oxman, Mary was not afforded any special consideration. Her professors were also immune to her sexual advances. One even threatened to go to her father.

*Damn them all she hell*, Mary thought. *I'll find another way.*

The answer came in the form of another student, Paul Craft. Paul was known around campus as the 'Candy Man.' He sold Mary a variety of narcotics: Amphetamines that kept her awake for all night study sessions, allowing her to stay hyper-focused; Quaaludes to help her crash. For partying purposes, she chose to ingest mescaline, and LSD. It was these hallucinogens that allowed her to escape the pressure associated with her studies.

At the end of her second semester, Danny said, "Excellent grades, Mary, but you'll have to do better in your philosophy course."

Mary popped an upper that night to cram for the next day's test. Her professor was impressed with her work, adding, "Interesting insight into the topic. Unique."

She had no recollection of what she had written.

"Thank you," she said. "I thought long and hard about what I wanted to say."

# CHAPTER 31

Mary had trouble in her social science classes. Too many unknowns. She did not believe in God. Darwin's theory of evolution was more up her alley. She was like her father that way. But what Mary cared about more than science was money. And the sooner she could get her hands on her trust fund the better. Mary had no grand plans to work for a living, not even at Oxman & Sons, Inc. even though her father dropped hints that she would take over the company one day. She only encouraged that sentiment to win her father's approval.

*But I must graduate Magnum Cum Laude*, Mary thought, popping a pill. *I must make sure daddy remains proud of me."*

Mary's drug use curbed her appetite. Slim in high school, she was ethereal by the time spring semester rolled around. She was not concerned, though. She actually reveled in her appearance, adoring the attention bestowed upon her by the wealthy young men she dated. They were forever complimenting her on her lithe body, every inch of it. Her parents, however, were not of the same mindset, at least her mother.

"I know Harvard is tough. I mean, I'm sure it is, but you need to take care of yourself too," Rose said, handing Mary a cup of chicken soup. "Eat."

"She needs to do whatever it takes to get through her studies," Danny countered. "Besides she's not malnourished."

He was concerned about Mary too, but he understood the rigors of studying in order to become a success. He was inordinately proud of his daughter's ambition.

Mary forced down the chicken soup, her hand trembling. She

would need a downer soon. Did she bring any home with her? She had trouble remembering. She managed to calm herself down though, because she knew her father always kept a supply of narcotics at home. If she needed to take a pill from the little black bag he stashed in his office closet, so be it.

Despite her lack of sleep and inadequate nutrition, Mary continued to keep her grades up thanks to the Candy Man. In her sophomore year she found that advanced chemistry was her favorite class, mostly because of Professor Douglas Stanton. He was in his early forties, strikingly handsome, and obviously excited about his tenured position. He tended to talk rapidly, using hand gestures to emphasis important points, and he was sexy as hell.

One day while listening to Professor Stanton lecture about various chemical compounds and their explosive properties, he started to melt. Mary squinted. Yes, the skin on his face was falling away. She saw his pulsing red cheek muscles, and sinewy ligaments underneath, and blood from his nose splashing onto the floor. His gray sweater unraveled exposing his naked chest. The first sighting of raw bone became apparent in his groin.

But even as he was melting right in front of the room, none of the other students seemed to notice. They were paying apt attention to him, some jotting notes. Mary shook her head, amazed that the man was able to continue talking, but then she realized his mouth was intact, and that his words were dancing in the air in bright orange lettering.

Mary felt her face flush, then she bolted upright from her chair, screaming, her eyes tightly closed. The next thing she knew people were gathered around her, their hands gripping her flailing arms, hurting her.

*"Don't you see?"* She shouted. *"Don't you get what's happening?"*

"Maybe she's having a seizure," Jill Graves said, then she heard Professor Stanton demand, "What's *wrong*, Ms. Oxman?"

Absolute terror invaded her body before Mary was able to open her eyes, looking directly into those of Professor Stanton. He was standing in front of her with a perfectly formed body, his sweater and tie intact.

"I…I, yes. I'm fine. Nothing's wrong."

Professor Stanton insisted Mary visit the campus nurse, but she brushed off his concern, explaining she was prone to sudden fits of panic attacks.

"All I need is some…some rest," she argued.

After a brief exchange, Professor Stanton relented. "Well, if you're *absolutely* certain, Ms. Oxman."

"Positive," Mary insisted.

"I suppose it would be all right if you go directly to your room." He looked up. "Ms. Graves, can you walk with her?"

"That won't be necessary," Mary said, moving away. "I'm fine. Really."

She felt everyone's eyes on her back as she hurried out of the room.

Instead of heading for the dorm though, Mary went to the campus library. In the reference section, she located a hard copy of *The Physician's Drug Reference Handbook.* Pulling the text from a high shelf – It felt heavy in her hands – she found an empty table, and began to flip through its pages. An hour later she closed the book, then stroked its smooth cover, horrified at what she learned.

Of course, Mary was familiar with the term 'flashback,' but she thought she was immune to such side effects. She was Mary Oxman, the daughter of one of America's richest families. She… she never thought something as awful as what she had just experienced could happen to *her*. Flashbacks happened to poor people; hopeless, homeless drug addicts on the streets, hungry, and cold, and unloved. Flashbacks simply did not happen to somebody of her financial, and educational status.

But it had.

That night she lay prone on her bed staring at the darkened ceiling of her dorm room, obsessing about what she had done to her body, worrying about the possibility of future episodes. When she finally fell asleep nightmares haunted her.

At Sunday brunch the next weekend Rose took one look at her daughter's face. She had been worried about Mary for quite some time, thinking that perhaps she was just going through a rough patch. Now the bags under her daughter's eyes, and her too-thin figure prompted her to say bluntly, "Mary, you look awful."

"Gee. Thanks mother."

Danny was slipping into his overcoat anxious to leave; he was late for a golf game at his country club.

"What are you talking about, Rose? She's fine. It's not easy taking classes at an Ivy League school, not that you would know anything about the rigors of earning a college education. Franklin paid your way through Vassar."

His words pierced Rose's heart, but this was not about her, this was about Mary.

"She needs to see a doctor," Rose insisted, folding her arms, thinking this was a fight Danny would not win. "She's studying herself into her grave."

"I *am* a doctor," Danny said, checking his Rolex. "If I felt something was wrong with her, I'd take steps to get her medical attention just like I did for James."

Mary stiffened at the mention of her brother's name. A memory of her small hands pressing the pillow against her brother's face that Christmas morning so many years ago filled her mind.

"You're fine, right?" Danny asked.

"Right," Mary said dully.

"See? Leave her alone, Rose. She's fine."

And without meaning to Rose snapped, "Just because *you* didn't make it into Harvard –

She stopped abruptly, studying her hands.

Mary knitted her brow, looking over at her father. She had no idea which universities he had attended; she had assumed Harvard since he was so gung-ho about wanting her to go there, and James before her.

Danny stormed out of the kitchen braying, "Leave her be, Rose. She's perfectly fine!"

And Mary thought, *I'm not fine, daddy. I'm not...*

# CHAPTER 32

Mary suffered two more flashbacks that exceeded the horror of her first ordeal, but despite the side effects of her drug use, Mary refused to stop using.

*I am an Oxman,* she told herself. *I will survive.*

Somehow Mary did survive. When she had been graduated from Harvard in the spring of 1982, her father threw an elaborate party for her. He invited the high society elite, and they all came to bestow congratulations upon Danny's only heir.

"What do you want to do now?" Danny asked the following day.

"She should stay home and recuperate from the last four years," Rose said, frowning.

"For once we agree mother," Mary said. "I do need a break, but I'm too restless to stay home."

Her parents were staring at her.

"What do you mean?" Danny asked as though she was speaking Chinese.

"Well, I would..." Mary looked from one to the other and continued, "Well, I would like to travel a bit on my own. Take a hiatus, so to speak. Like, for a year."

Her father mulled over the idea. He wanted her to work in a lab at Oxman & Sons, Inc., get some experience before moving up in the company.

Mary gazed into her father's eyes, and she said something she had not planned. "Graduate school. I'd like to go to graduate school," she blurted out.

Danny's facial features softened. "Oh. Any school in particular?"

"She should stay home and rest," Rose sniffed. "Graduate school is *not* taking a break."

Mary thought about one of her friends, Olivia Joahnson, who was all excited about studying abroad at…at…and then she remembered.

"Ecole Normale Superieure," Mary said.

"Paris?" Rose said uneasily.

"Like I said, I think it would be helpful for me if I had a change of scenery. You know, had an opportunity for a new study abroad experience. Don't you agree, daddy?"

Danny considered this. After all, Mary was growing up, becoming an independent woman in her own right. Studying abroad would be a good experience for her. Besides, Mary's absence would result in more loneliness for Rose, which would serve as further punishment for his wife's infidelity.

"Yes. Yes, I do," he said, nodding.

Rose sighed, knowing that once again she would not win. She knew how much Danny valued education. And the more education their daughter received, the closer she became to taking over Oman & Sons, Inc. She sighed, listening as her husband and daughter made plans.

Mary left for France the following fall.

Danny sent his daughter off to Europe on his private jet where she was to live in a luxurious high-rise security apartment in an upscale neighborhood of Quartier Latin. Upon her arrival, Mary was met by a part-time maid, and a cook.

"The hired help will allow you more time to study, so you won't have to worry about minutiae," Danny had explained before Mary left.

"And you'll be forced to eat better food," her mother added.

Mary rolled her eyes, secretly pleased. "I'll be fine," she said.

Mary had visited Paris before during overseas trips in high school and had fallen in love with the city of lights then. That feeling did not change now. When she did eat, French food pleased her palate, as did all the men she met. There were so many to choose from too: Struggling artists and writers and wanna-be famous entertainers. These were the men Mary felt most attracted to, not the uppity, tight ass Harvard types that you brought home to meet your parents.

During her first semester, Mary had been good about keeping up with her class work like she had promised her father. Then, just before Christmas vacation, she met a Frenchman, and that's when Mary's life turned upside down.

The man was a day laborer, eight years her senior. They met at a small out-of-the-way café. Mary bumped into him by accident – literally – spilling the glass of red wine she held onto her winter white Vera Wang dress.

"*Ooohhh*, I am so sorry, Cheri," the man said.

Mary frowned, swiping at the stain with a bar napkin. She started to move along when she felt a hand on her arm, and then she looked up into the eyes of a stranger; a striking man who took her breath away.

The man was tall, and muscular, with dark hair and gold speckled green eyes. He had a strong chin; a chain of sparkling white teeth, and a smile to die for.

"I'm afraid I will have to pick up your cleaning tab for helping you spill that wine on your lovely dress. Here. Let me buy you another drink," he offered.

Almost against her will, Mary followed him to the bar.

Over drinks he told her his name in a light French accent: John Paul Chantel. He explained in vivid detail his dreams of wanting to become an important film producer.

"You speak English very well," Mary observed.

"*Ahhh,* I have been to America on many occasions. Hollywood. I go there to check out business investors. People who have money to help me pay for my dream. It is not easy, Cheri. I am afraid I do not have the money for... how do you say? Backing?

For my movies. But I will find people to help me. I am saving all my pennies, as you Americans say. I work on my English, so in California they will know how serious I am about my work." His eyes bored into hers.

Mesmerized, Mary listened intently to his stories. While John Paul asked her questions about her own life, Mary held back. She had no intention of scaring him off with talk about the colorful Oxman clan. Besides, she liked the feeling of normalcy; of anonymity.  Since she was a child, Mary had known that most people she met pretended to like her because of the Oxman prestige. Through the years her father taught her to "trust no one," and Mary took that advice to heart as she grew older. Now, Mary felt like any other struggling college grad student studying abroad, even in the Vera Wang dress.

After that first night, the two started to date. Mary wanted to have sex with John Paul during their first week together; her body burned with desire, but surprisingly it was he who held back.

"I do not make love to a woman unless *I* am in love with her," he told her earnestly.

He was the most sincere person Mary had ever met.

John Paul and Mary soon became an item. He liked her friends, although he did not introduce her to his.

"They are different from your friends at university," he said. "When it is time, you will meet them. Besides I am many years older than you. I am afraid my friends would bore you to tears. I am impressed with you being young, and with the schooling you are getting here. That is not my -

"Don't be," Mary interrupted.

John Paul frowned. "My parents are poor, Cheri. I had no chance to go to university. No money," he said, shrugging. "Now, here I am at thirty-three years old working odd construction jobs." His voice was tinged with sadness.

Mary's heart went out to him.

"I have loans up my ass," she lied.

"Then why is your apartment so expensive, Cheri?" John Paul asked, throwing his denim jacket onto her sofa, admiring the living room with its gleaming hardwood flooring, and stone fireplace.

Mary was ready for this question. "I have an aunt who is rich, rich. She owns this building, and she -

"There is need to explain," John Paul assured her, smiling. "There is an explanation for all that happens to us, Oui?"

Mary's body was on fire. "Oui," she agreed, hugging him close.

Two months later as they walked along the River Seine hand in hand, John Paul suddenly twirled her around almost knocking her off her feet as she laughed.

"I am in love with you, Mary," he declared.

"Me too," she gushed.

"You are in love with you?" John Paul teased, kissing her before she could respond.

That night they had gone to bed together for the first time. John Paul was the most experienced lover Mary had ever had, thoughtful and caring about her pleasure, embracing her gently, murmuring into her ear that he wanted to please her, and he did...over and over again.

Early one morning a few weeks later, the phone on the night table jangled, waking Mary. Lying next to her John Paul rolled over in bed. A light rain beat against the window panes.

"Hello?" Mary rasped, turning away so as not to disturb him.

"How are you, darling?"

At the sound of her father's voice, Mary perked up.

"Fabulous. I adore France," she said, clearing her throat, getting up on one elbow, trying to remember what day it was. "I mean, what I am learning here is getting more interesting every day," she clarified, which was partly true anyway. John Paul had just spent the night teaching Mary sexual antics she had never known existed.

"What classes are your taking?" her mother asked on the extension. "Ah, Spring in Paris. How exciting!"

After meeting John Paul, Mary had not been attending classes regularly; as a matter of fact, she was certain she was failing biochemistry, but now she said, "Good. You know, like Harvard good."

"I'm glad," Danny said. "Well, if you need anything Mary, let me know."

He sounded anxious, like he wanted to get off the phone. So did Mary. John Paul had turned onto his side, rustling the bed covers, his hard-on pushing playfully at the small of her back.

"Don't worry. I have everything I need at the moment," Mary said with a grin.

She hung up as John Paul was tying the wrist of her free hand to the bed post while Mary pretended to struggle.

Soon after that the two became inseparable with John Paul spending most of his days after work at her apartment.

"I want to see where you live," Mary pouted over a candlelight dinner at her apartment one evening. The cook had prepared an excellent meal, leaving just before John Paul arrived. He had no clue about the hired help.

"You will," he said evasively. "This meat is delicious. What is it?"

Mary had no idea. "Veal," she guessed.

"Veal. Nice. You are a good cook."

They had white wine with dinner, but Mary did not overdo. She was proud of herself for not indulging too much since she and John Paul had become exclusive. Paul knew of Mary's drug laden background, although she had not revealed the details of her flashbacks, realizing she had not suffered from one in over a year, thank God.

"I was a kid making stupid choices," she had explained. "Doesn't everybody?"

"Some," John Paul agreed. He looked away so Mary could not see his eyes. "Some of us, yes Cheri."

On the way back to Mary's apartment John Paul said, "I want you to do something for me. Very important. Would you?"

"That depends. What?"

John Paul sat her down, and explained in vivid detail.

The idea instantly intrigued her, and the fact she loved him made it that much easier to agree.

"Okay," she said. "But just this once, darling. I will do this once. For you."

"Oui, that is all I need," he said, rewarding her with a brilliant smile.

"I love you, John Paul," Mary said, realizing she had never uttered those words to any other man.

His eyes shone. "I love you too, Mary," he said. "More than you can ever imagine."

# CHAPTER 33

When most people think of Paris, they visualize the Eiffel Tower; cobble stone streets; quaint flower shops, and artists working on oil paintings while studying lovely countryside landscapes. Part of this vision is true, of course, but the other half fiction. There is a dark side of Paris too, where the poor reside in decaying apartment buildings; desperate for survival, scamming tourists, burglarizing the wealthy, and worse.

John Paul lived in such a neighborhood, specifically in an illegal loft located in the suburbs of France a few miles from the Peripherique.

"I know that my place is not what you are used to, Cheri," John Paul said apologetically as they walked along the cracked sidewalk.

An old woman wearing a knit cap, and woolen coat despite the heat, stood on one corner. She had a deeply wrinkled face, and swollen ankles, and wore tattered shoes.

"Here Martha," John Paul said, carelessly throwing coins into her tin cup.

The old woman grabbed his hand, kissing the top of it, muttering something in French that Mary could not understand. And then something strange happened. Martha moved passed John Paul and took one of Mary's hands in hers, squeezing it tightly for a moment before letting go. The old woman looked as though she were about to say something to Mary, then put an index finger to her cracked lips.

Mary knitted her brow staring into Martha's bloodshot eyes, then noticed John Paul had already started across the street beckoning, "Come on. My building is over here, Cheri."

When Mary turned back the old woman was gone.

Mary followed John Paul inside a mill building where she was assaulted with the smell of something rotting. There was dark graffiti on the walls in the cramped hallway, save for a crude painting of a pink octopus with long flowing tentacles that reminded Mary of the first time she had ingested mescaline another lifetime ago.

A child, no more than four years old, was crouched near the stairwell inspecting something unseen on the worn carpeting, humming. She did not look up when John Paul and Mary walked around her.

Mary was beginning to think it was not the best idea to come here, but after they had climbed the stairs to the top floor – the rickety gated elevator was out of order – and entered John Paul's loft, Mary looked around at the simply decorated space, and breathed, "This is *surreal*."

The loft was open air with high ceilings and hanging fans and newly painted walls, and tasteful black and white leather furniture. Checkered scattered rugs were strewn everywhere. A light scent of musk lingered in the air, delighting Mary's senses.

John Paul said with obvious pride, "I worked hard to get my place to look good, Cheri," he said, smiling his brilliant smile. "Here, let me give you, how do you say, the best tour."

"The grand tour," Mary corrected.

The kitchen was small, but neat, with white cabinets and a simple counter top. There was a tiny, but immaculate bathroom, and the bedroom was divine. The walls were painted a soft white, and sported gold-framed photographs, crude but tasteful; naked women in various poses, artistically beautiful.

Strangely, there was no other furniture in the bedroom with its makeshift walls, save for a kind-sized bed. The dark cherry wood headboard looked like someone had hand-carved it with intricate geometrical designs. The mattress was covered in a black quilt that shimmered from floor lamps casting their warm glow around the area.

"I...there are no words," Mary said in awe. "This place is... well, like any *normal* apartment."

John Paul laughed, obviously pleased. "Come. We will have wine, oui?"

"Red. Yes, please." Mary said, following him back into the living space where she perched on a black futon cushion.

The person John Paul wanted her to meet arrived soon after the tour. The woman was beyond beautiful with long dark hair that cascaded to her waist. She was short and slender, so petite she looked as though she could fly away. Her eyes were large, brown and long lashed, and she had flawless skin. Her lips were pink and full. Mary looked closely at the other woman's face and could see she wore no makeup.

"This is my dear friend, Adele," John Paul said.

Mary felt a stab of jealously. She was coming up on her twenty fourth birthday, and Adele looked no more than eighteen, making Mary feel old.

"Is she legal?" Mary asked, as though Adele was not in the room.

John Paul grimaced. "Of course! I am not a pedophile, Cheri."

"I didn't mean to imply..." Mary began, then swallowed, but the thrill of what she was about to do transcended her jealously. Besides, she had promised him this favor, and she was desperate to keep him happy. John Paul had said he loved her. No man had ever loved her before.

She would do this one thing for him, and that would be the end of that.

***

"Wow!" Mary said.

"Wow," John Paul repeated.

"Incredible," Mary said.

"Incredible," John Paul agreed.

Adele had gone hours before, and since then Mary and John Paul made love three times, napping in between. Reluctantly, they arose around 8:00 p.m.

"Are you hungry, Cheri? I can ring some friends and we can meet at a little café close by. You will like, yes?"

Finally, he wanted her to meet his friends!

"That sounds like fun," Mary said.

As they dressed, she studied John Paul buttoning his shirt, and heard herself say, "I want you to meet my parents."

"But they are in America." He paused, adjusting his belt. "Besides they would not like me."

Mary tilted her head, puzzled. "Why not?"

John Paul avoided her eyes, and then she realized. "Oh, John Paul!" she said. "My parents will not care if you are a construction worker. They will be impressed with your um, ambition, even though they don't need the details," Mary said, already thinking about the lie she would tell them about John Paul's career.

"I have no money to fly to America," John Paul hedged.

Mary started to say, *That won't be a problem. My father will send his private jet,* but then she remembered John Paul did not know about her background. Perhaps now was the time to explain, but he had already left the room. The moment for doing so passed.

# CHAPTER 34

John Paul and Mary walked hand in hand to a café a few blocks away called the *Squealing Hog*; a hole in the wall kind of place, very European, dark and cave-like with stone walls and dim lighting. The place smelled like beer and raw fish. It was late; the place was jam packed, and noisy.

They found a table near the bar, and were studying their menus when a woman's voice rang out, "John Paul, darling! *There* you are."

Not a woman Mary saw, a man. He was small-boned and effeminate, with a mop of curly hair and luminescent eyes. He wore a bright pink scarf and tight jeans. He took the seat next to Mary.

"Is this she?" He said, taking Mary's hand in his, which felt soft and damp in hers. "She is lovely. Just *lovely*."

"Yes, this is my Mary," John Paul said proudly, and she smiled at the use of the pronoun 'my.' "Mary, this is my good friend, Peppie."

Another man sidled up to the table, tall and harsh looking with close cropped hair, and acne scarred skin. He wore a diamond stud earring, and had a sleeve of tattoos running along both of his bare arms. Apparently, he was not as impressed with Mary as Peppie. He barely acknowledged her when John Paul said, "And this is Malachi."

Malachi leaned towards John Paul, ignoring the others. "We gotta talk."

Mary tried to overhear the conversation, but Peppie kept chirping in her ear, and so was not able to.

"And then that nasty, *nasty* woman never thought I could pull off that photo shoot!" Peppie complained." I swear on my dead papa's body, God bless his soul, these images will wind up in an important magazine one day. Mary? Are you listening?"

But Mary wasn't.  She was thinking about what John Paul had told her months before.

*My friends are different than yours from university.*

John Paul tried to get the attention of a server, but the woman bustled by their table balancing a tray above their heads, ignoring him.

Finally, John Paul rose. "I'll get us drinks," he announced, and Malachi stood up to go with him.

A band started to play; the cacophony of the loud music caused Mary to begin to get the onset of a headache, as Peppie babbled on about things she did not quite understand. She was glad to see the other men return. Malachi, holding two mugs in his hands, set one before Peppie, the other at his place. Mary did not drink beer, so John Paul put the mug he held in front of his seat, and handed her a tall glass filled with a turquoise liquid with bits of pineapple bobbing amongst ice cubes.

"What's this?" She asked, sipping. The drink was sweet with a bitter edge. Different.

"A specialty of the house," John Paul said, and for a moment he sounded American. Mary drank, hoping the liquid would calm her nerves. Amazingly it did. John Paul brought her another when she finished, but warned, "Don't drink this one too fast, Cheri. It's like a devil's potion."

Malachi eyed him. "Good choice of words," he said.

Mary did not heed the warning. She drank two thirds of what was in the glass in less than five minutes.

Finally, a server came to take their order, but Mary's appetite had vanished. The combination of the smell of raw fish, the loud music, and her drinks, made her stomach feel woozy.

"I need to use the loo," she announced suddenly, bolting out of her chair, then pushing her way through the crowd to the bathroom, where she leaned against a wall while waiting in line. Finally, a stall door opened, and a woman stepped out, strikingly beautiful. She looked out of place here, like she belonged in an elegant restaurant with white table cloths and candlelight; a place that served expensive food, and offered soft music to an upper-class crowd. For a moment, their eyes met. Mary thought she recognized the woman, but could not place her.

When Mary was done using the toilet, and washing her hands, she returned to the table, almost falling into her chair as a wave of dizziness washed over her.

"Oh, Cheri. Enough for you," John Paul admonished as Malachi stared at her, disparagingly. Everything about him reeked. She so desperately wanted to get out of there.

The server appeared balancing two plates of raw little necks on the half shell.

The second Mary saw the appetizers, she turned her head, and vomited onto the floor.

Then she passed out cold.

# CHAPTER 35

The next morning Mary awoke in her own bed. She was alone lying under the Egyptian cotton sheets, naked. A beam of sunlight was streaking into the window, spilling onto her face.

Mary squinted at the nightstand clock: Friday, April 27th, 11:07 a.m.

*Friday.*

She had missed her biochemistry class. *Damn!*

And that's when it hit her. She had been with John Paul at his loft the night before, and then they had gone out to a dark, noisy café, and she had…

The memories flooded back.

"Oh, my God," she said aloud, visualizing herself projectile vomiting, and then…nothing.

She got out of bed, slowly, her heading pounding; stomach queasy. She thought she would vomit again, but took a few deep breaths and the feeling eased. She dressed in jeans and a black tee then went in search of John Paul, feeling terribly embarrassed about what had happened.

"John Paul?" Mary called, checking the bathroom, the kitchen, and even the spare bedroom, even though she sensed she was alone.

*Maybe he left a note, not that he had ever done that before,* she thought.

But then again, he had never just left her alone in the morning like this after a night out together either. Or had he *not* stayed? Now that she thought about it, how did she get home? She didn't remember anything that had happened after she passed out. She looked around for a note, but found none.

In the kitchen she poured herself a half glass of water and drank it slowly, then went into the bathroom, used the toilet, washed her hands, then brushed her teeth, thinking that John Paul had to have driven her home; his friends would have no clue where she lived.

*He's pissed off because I embarrassed him and so he brought me here then left,* she thought, and the accompanying feelings of embarrassment and shame tripled before suddenly switching to feelings of rage.

*It's like I care about what a man thinks of me! Like I need to be forgiven by John Paul for drinking too much*, she thought, and that realization made her livid with all this negative emotion flowing through her and directed at *herself,* because she had never cared about what any man had thought about her before…until now. Until she had met John Paul Chantel, and had fallen madly in love with him.

Mary tried calling his home number. There was no answer, nor did his machine pick up. After ten rings, she reluctantly replaced the receiver, thought a moment, then pulled out the phone directory. Tapping one index finger lightly against her lips, she tried to remember the name of the construction company where he worked.

*Ah, yes*, she thought, when her eyes fell upon a familiar company name.

Mary hesitated.

*I hate to call him at work, but under the circumstances –*

The phone rang while she was pondering her decision.

She snatched up the receiver.

"John Paul?" She said, but it was her friend Meredith, wanting to know why she missed her biochem class.

"I overslept."

"Well, Professor Regis was really pissed," Meredith told her.

"I'm not surprised," Mary said. I'm barely making it through his class as it is." She put a palm against her forehead. "Hey, did you hear from John Paul by any chance?"

"No. Why? I don't really talk to him unless you're with him," she answered quickly. Too quickly? "You okay, Mary?"

"Fine. I can't talk right now, though. Gotta get to my afternoon classes. Later okay?"

Mary hung up, thinking that maybe she didn't pass out after all, that maybe she suffered another flashback instead. But even if that was the case, surely John Paul would not have left her home alone under that circumstance either.

Making a decision, Mary pressed her left index finger against a page of the phone book, memorized the number, and dialed. After two rings, a woman answered.

"Bondia. Myrex.".

In her best French, Mary asked for John Paul Chantel.

"*Qui?*"

Mary felt her heart drop. "John Paul Chantel. He works at your company," she said, lapsing into English, and then repeated, "Il travaille chez vous," hoping she got that right.

"*Je suis desole. Je pense que vous avez le mauvais numero.*" The woman replied.

Mary wrinkled her brow, and thought, *Wrong phone number my ass*, then said, "John Paul Chantel –

"No Mademoiselle. Je suis desole. Personne par ce nom ne travaille ici," the woman said, and hung up.

*No one by that name…* Mary mused letting the receiver drop back into the cradle.

She decided she had called the wrong company. She made a mental note to ask John Paul later where he worked, and they would laugh over her mistake.

"Yes, later," she said aloud.

Mary went to her afternoon chemistry lab, but had trouble concentrating. She managed to stay though until class let out, when she realized she was mildly hungry. At any rate, eating something would probably calm her stomach, and steady her hands. She went to the cafeteria where she found Meredith sitting at a table by herself.

"Hey, Mary, what's up?" She said. "You look awful."

"I haven't heard from John Paul all day." The words flew out, unbidden.

Meredith stuck the tines of a fork into her garden salad laughing. "All *day*? Wow. That's like, what? A whole six hours?"

"I don't need sarcasm right now," Mary snapped. "It's… complicated. He…he didn't stay at my place last night, and that has never happened before. We're *always* together."

Meredith looked at her, and there was something in her eyes that made Mary uneasy.

"Well, he is French, after all," Meredith said, her voice low.

Mary stiffened. "What does *that* mean?"

Meredith put her fork on the table, and pursed her lips. "Oh, man! None of us wanted to tell you," she said, averting Mary's eyes.

"Tell me *what*?"

"I don't," she began, stopped, considered, then continued. "That John Paul is…" He…oh nothing. Forget it. I'm a fool."

"No, tell me!" Mary insisted.

Meredith glanced around at the nearly empty cafeteria. Reluctantly, she looked into Mary's eyes, then said bluntly, "John Paul has asked me out at least half a dozen times over the last month alone. Of course, I said no. I would never -

"You're lying," Mary hissed.

"No," Meredith fidgeted in her chair. "None of us wanted to tell you."

*Us?*

The pronoun hung in the air, while Mary processed that one word. "You lying *bitch*," she snapped.

Meredith raised her eyebrows.

"I'm not lying," she said stiffly. "John Paul made the moves on Joanie Rivet too."

"What the hell are you talking about?" Mary said, feeling her world start to crumble.

And Alicien Klienburg. We… none of us wanted to tell you, Mary. Well actually we thought you *knew,* and simply didn't care. We thought –

"Shut up!" Mary snapped. "You're all jealous because John Paul Chantel is with *me*, and not any of you *lying cunts*."

Mary saw a flash of anger in Meredith's dark eyes as she rose to her feet, placed both palms on the cafeteria table, leaned forward, and snapped, "Mary Oxman you are a complete, self-centered *bitch*. We didn't want to tell you *that* either."

On the way home Mary seethed. How dare Meredith tell her such an obvious lie? They were supposed to be *friends*. Besides, everyone knew she and John Paul was an item. The hot couple around town.

*Those bitches are just jealous*, Mary decided. *Who needs them?*

But when Mary returned to her apartment, John Paul was not there waiting for her.

In spite of herself she thought, *Is he in bed with Joanie Rivet right now?*

The stab of fear in her chest returned.

# CHAPTER 36

John Paul failed to get in touch with Mary over the weekend. She left phone messages on his answering machine, but when they went unanswered, called hospitals, thinking that he lay in a coma after a terrible accident, but nothing was amiss. She frequented restaurants and bars where they typically hung out together, even hoping to spot Peppie or Malachi at *The Squealing Hog*, but was unsuccessful. It seemed as if John Paul Chantel had vanished into thin air.

Mary waited out the weekend alone, vacillating between anger and worry as time passed agonizingly slowly. She didn't eat, drink, or shower, sick with worry and shame of having had made a fool of herself at the *Squealing Hog*, and embarrassing John Paul to the point that he didn't want to see her.

*This is how terminally ill people must feel as they await death,* she thought.

On Monday, she forced herself to shower, downed a cup of bitter coffee, and ate part of a stale blueberry muffin, then headed to her bio chemistry class in an effort to forget John Paul's looming absence, at least for a couple of hours.

As it turned out, Professor Atkins was late. Just as the students tired of waiting and were packing up to leave, he arrived out of breath.

"Sorry. Got stuck in traffic," he explained, and popped open a briefcase. Mary settled back into her seat. A few minutes later Professor Atkins was looming over her.

*Shit. He's pissed I didn't show up Friday,* Mary thought.

She quickly thought of an excuse, but he surprised her by saying, "I received word that Amelia St. Pierre wants to see you."

Why would the university president want to see me?"

"I have no idea," Professor Atkins replied. He returned to the front of the room, and when he saw that Mary was still seated said, "I guess I wasn't clear. Ms. St. Pierre wants to see you *now*."

*Oh God, I'm probably failing out of school. My father is going to kill me.*

Mary felt out of kilter somehow; out of control. It was an alien feeling for her; one she didn't like. She left the classroom, and made her way towards the president's office across campus, trying to figure out why she was being summoned, convinced it was because of her poor grades, but then another, more realistic thought surfaced.

*Ah yes. My father probably gave the school a generous donation, and she wants to thank me in person*, Mary thought. It wouldn't be the first time a similar situation had occurred through the years.

The office of the president was located in a lovely red brick building with snakes of ivy crawling up one side in a dozen different directions, reminding Mary of her Harvard years. She took the winding staircase to the third floor, and entered the reception area. She had been here once before when Amelia first met Mary and her father when Mary had initially been accepted to the university. The secretary, Ms. Brille, nodded toward a high-backed wing chair, and said cordially, "Ms. Pierre will see you momentarily, Ms. Oxman."

*She wants me to actually wait for her*? Mary thought amazed, and then decided, out of respect for her father and his generous donation to the school, to cooperate.

Mary sat, and noticed a silver pot of coffee, and a platter of croissants spread out on a round table a few feet away. Ms. Brille went back to her paperwork without asking if Mary wanted anything.

*Rude!*

What was even ruder was the fifteen minutes that passed without another word from Ms. Brille, or the appearance of Amelia St. Pierre. Mary was not used to waiting for anyone. *She* was the one who people waited for. After another few minutes of sitting and fuming – she at least had to explain to her father she *did* wait - she got to her feet when Ms. Brille's phone buzzed.

"Ms. St. Pierre will see you now," she announced.

Mary noted Ms. Brille did not get up to escort her to the office. Disturbed, Mary rose and opened the heavy oak door herself.

Amelia St. Pierre sat behind an impressive oak desk. There was floor to ceiling book cases behind her, and expensive rugs scattered on the floor, and windows everywhere with magnificent views of a sprawling English garden behind the building. Picture perfect.

"Ah, Mary. Shut the door. Thank you for coming," Ameila said, her voice warm.

Mary closed the door behind her, which latched shut with a soft clicking sound.

"So sorry to have kept you waiting. Busy, busy. You understand."

Several windows were open, letting in the smell of tulips and Sweet Pea, and honey suckle. Mary noted several wall paintings that could never be mistaken for imitations. She spotted a Monet right off.

Amelia St. Pierre was an enigma around campus, rarely seen, and hardly heard from. She was young, ambitious, and an exceptionally beautiful brunette, with large blue eyes, and a marionette nose. She was said to rule the university staff with an iron fist, especially keeping every faculty member in line, even those with tenure.

"Have a seat Ms. Oxman," Amelia offered, graciously. "Would you like tea? Soda?"

Mary chose a rose patterned chintz chair, sat and crossed her legs, more anxious to get out of there than curious to know what this woman wanted with her. A cool spring wind blew across the room causing tiny goose bumps to form on Mary's forearms.

"Nothing, thanks. What can I do for you?" She said without fanfare.

Amelia's smile widened. The paintings may not be imitations, Mary thought, but those teeth had to be – veneer.

Amelia studied the young woman before her, feeling a momentary stab of pity, which vanished as quickly as it had come. She had not discussed what she was about to bring up with anyone, not even her husband, Peter. Not that they spoke much these days anyway. She had plans to divorce him.

"Your father is a generous man," Amelia began. "He donates money freely to our institution and many others in the states. Hundreds of thousands of dollars through the years."

So, Mary had been right after all. Well, she would listen to the woman's rambling thank you, and be gone.

Amelia paused, scratching behind an earlobe that sported an emerald stud. "We want to keep him happy. Oui?

"Of course," Mary said.

"Of course," Amelia repeated. "That's why I have, what do you Americans, say? A deleema."

"Oh? What kind?" Mary asked.

*God, she wants even more money. Greedy bitch*, Mary thought.

Amelia pouted, her plump lips puffed.

"I am afraid your papa would not be so happy if he knew what you have been doing here, Mary." She wagged an index finger in the air, her bright red-tipped nail serving as a stop sign. "No, no. Mademoiselle."

Suddenly, Amelia St. Pierre had Mary's full attention.

"I have some information for you, oui? Something for you to see. To *think* about, Mary." The toothy smiled returned. "But I am afraid it will not make you very happy."

# CHAPTER 37

Mary stared at Amelia warily.

"What are you talking about? I thought –

A side door opened. Both women turned their heads, and Mary's jaw dropped open.

John Paul Chantel came into the room, pushing a gray metal cart with a television on top. He stopped a yard away from Amelia's desk, and smiled his magnificent smile at her, then at Mary, as if Mary was an afterthought.

"John Paul! What are –

Confusion filled Mary's brain. She thought she was experiencing a flashback, but no. John Paul was real flesh and blood, standing right there in front of her. Mary's blood ran cold.

"Mary," John Paul said graciously, before turning and plugging the end of the television cord into a wall socket. Amelia got up, positioning the screen.

"Is this good, Mary. Can you see?" She asked.

But Mary didn't *want* to see. She wanted to flee, but she couldn't move. It was as though someone else had inhabited her body, and she was watching the scene unfold in front of her through that person's eyes; a calm, detached person.

John Paul turned on the television, and Mary couldn't help but watch the movie that unfolded before her eyes; at the performance of the actors that were doing unspeakable things to each other.

*No, not actors*, she thought with horror. Mary leaned forward, her eyes glued to the screen as she watched images of herself and

John Paul, standing naked in the bedroom in his loft. They were French kissing – how ironic! - While each other's hands explored the crevices of the other's most intimate places, their faces without a doubt recognizable.

And then, of course, Adele walked into the room. She was naked too, with her perky breasts and tight ass in plain view, and John Paul stepped aside as the younger woman allowed Mary to push her playfully onto the mattress with the exquisite headboard - *Hand carved* - Mary now thought crazily- and then Adele started to do things to her body that Mary remembered brought her instant pleasure, as John Paul filmed the entire scene from the corner of the room…with Mary's permission!

*I want to be an important film producer.*

*I want to help make that happen, John Paul.*

*…Ah, then There is something you can do for me, oui, Mary?*

And she had foolishly agreed! Because she loved him.

"This is outrageous!" Mary started to protest.

*I've been to America on many occasions. Hollywood, Cheri. I go there to check out business investors. People who have money to help me pay for my dream.*

So, John Paul had known all along about Mary Oxman and her family fortune!

"Enough!" Mary said, holding up a hand, shielding her eyes, the images still sequencing in her mind's eye.

John Paul turned off the television. Mary heard laughter drift into the room from outside: Students going to and from classes. Laughing at *her*!

John Paul strode up to Amelia, and she rose, and they embraced and kissed while Mary watched, her face turning bright red. Then they broke apart, and turned towards Mary in unison, and Amelia purred, "John Paul and I enjoy watching this film in bed. He always gets so, how do you say? Horny, every time."

The age-old finger of jealousy snaked inside of Mary at the same moment she suddenly recognized Amelia St. Pierre.

She had been the woman Mary spotted in the bathroom at the *Squealing Hog*. The one she thought didn't belong in a hole in the wall place like that.

Suddenly, Mary's jealously turned into rage that boiled up inside of her. Her eyes scanned the desk in front of her, zeroing in on a crystal paperweight, which she wanted to use to bash their skulls in.

"You would like to kill us,,, oui?" Amelia said. as if reading Mary's mind. "Ah, yes. But you will not. No. Because who knows what happened to poor little Miss Adele? She has been reported missing by her family. So sad."

Mary's heart dropped. She remembered the dark purple silk scarf John Paul had handed her off camera while she straddled Adele. She visualized wrapping the soft material around Adele's slim neck, pulling both ends outward as John Paul had instructed.

At first, Adele only smiled up at Mary, licking her lower pink lip. Then as directed by John Paul's hand gestures Mary pulled the silk ends more tightly, clearly remembering the panic in Adele's eyes that momentarily made Mary think about James, and what his face must have looked like under the pillow she had used to suffocate him. Adele's eyes bulged pleadingly up at Mary, her face gaining a purplish tint that almost matched the color of the scarf, while she arched her back, her eyes finally rolling upwards in their sockets with only the whites showing. Mary remembered she wanted to stop at that point, but John Paul had explained snuff films were only meant to look real.

"Adele is a pro at this. She'll be fine," he had assured her.

Of course, there was no reason for Mary to doubt him. She loved him; trusted him. And so, she did his bidding.

Finally, after what seemed an eternity, John Paul sliced his fingers across his throat. Mary let the scarf ends go free, but was it in time? Adele's eyes were closed; her facial and neck coloring bluish gray, and she lay very, very still.

John Paul turned off the camera, then scooped Adele up in his arms, saying he would revive her in the other room, not to worry. Minutes passed while Mary waited, and then he came back, sans Adele.

"Is she…? Mary was going to say 'dead,' but instead she said, "All right?"

John Paul smiled with delight. "She will have to wear that beautiful purple scarf to cover some bruises for a week or so, but oui. She is good," John Paul assured her. "I told you. This is not Adele's first time doing this type of film. She loves it."

Mary forced herself back to the present. Amelia was talking.

"It could be that Adele is dead, that you murdered her Mary, and if that's the case…she shrugged. "Well, in murder investigations evidence speaks for itself." She reached into a drawer, pulling out a plastic bag stuffed with purple colored fabric.

"What do you want?" Mary demanded.

"Two million dollars."

"I don't have them much."

"Your money is in trust. You are over twenty-one. You can access your account. Take as much money as you like."

"My father will ask questions."

"We know you can handle him."

Mary stiffened. "No."

Amelia sighed, leaning forward, her hands playing with the crystal paperweight. It gave off rays of rainbow colors upon the walls.

"Oh well, Cheri. Then it would be my duty to send a copy of this film to the policia. There are many copies, you understand." The smile returned. Mary wanted to break every one of those shiny teeth. She studied Amelia's calm expression, weighing her options carefully before realizing she had none.

With a great effort of sheer will Mary said, "I will make the arrangements."

Amelia nodded, scratching the side of her neck.

"That is an excellent choice," John Paul said, and Mary noted he sounded very American.

Mary used the armrests to push herself up from the chair, thinking she would deal with John Paul at a later date.

"I will be in touch," Amelia said, as Mary walked out of the office, her back perfectly straight.

# CHAPTER 38

The following morning after a sleepless night, Mary took a cab to John Paul's loft. She had to confront him.

But when she arrived, she saw that the entire building was under construction. Workers were placing bright orange cones around the perimeter. There were tractors everywhere, and men wearing yellow hard hats, one drilling the sidewalk near the front stairs.

Mary strode up to him. "Who is in charge?" She yelled over the noise.

The man stopped drilling, removing his ear protection.

"*What?*" He said in French.

"*I said who is in charge?*"

The man pointed to a hefty man across the street. Mary marched over to him.

"What is going on here?" She demanded, lips pursed.

The foreman studied the beautiful young woman before him. She was petite, and blonde, and wore expensive clothing, and surely did not belong in this neighborhood.

"You are American, yes?"

Mary immediately sensed his dislike of her. She nodded.

"Ah, then maybe you do not know. We are demolishing this building."

"But you can't!" She said. "There's someone living in there!"

"No, Mademoiselle. This building is empty."

"That's not true! There's a loft on the top floor!. Someone lives there," Mary said, turning to point.

"You are mistaken, Mademoiselle. These buildings have been vacant for the last six months."

He motioned for the man with the drill to begin work again. A *rat-tat-tat-tat* filled the air, hurting Mary's ears.

*"No. No! I will show you,"* Mary yelled, turning and racing inside the building.

The elevator still had the *Out of Order* sign tacked onto its rusted gate. Mary flew up the stairs, and when she arrived at John Paul's loft out of breath, she saw that the place *was* empty. Totally abandoned; the furniture, rugs, curtains…all gone except for some graffiti on the walls in black spray paint. One word caught her eye, almost indistinguishable.

*Sucker.*

Mary strode into the bedroom as the foreman appeared behind her.

*"Mademoiselle!* It is not safe to be here," he said, gulping air. "I told you no one -

Mary did not bother to respond. She turned, and fled.

Shaking his head, the foreman thought, *Crazy Americans.*

***

Mary spent the next few days on the party scene. A part of her hoped she would run into John Paul, but she had a feeling that would be a fail. He had disappeared again, so she decided to make it her life's work to find him, and punish him for what he had done to her.

To sleep she took pills, to stay awake she took pills, to get back to her studies, so as not to disappoint her father, Mary took more pills.

Nearly two months passed. Mary hardly slept, she barely ate, and she stopped attending classes. Meredith and her other friends had long since abandoned her.

And then one morning, half drugged, and sitting on the toilet, Mary heard a key turn in the front door lock of her apartment.

*John Paul!* She thought, wishing she was wearing makeup, and her hair was combed so she could properly tear him to pieces. Or maybe he had a change of heart and had come to apologize, and to explain that Amelia had forced him to turn over that horrid film. and they would hug and make plans to get their revenge together, instead of Mary having to smash his face in.

But when she finished with the toilet, and stumbled into the foyer in her black bathrobe, she found a surprise visitor standing there staring at her with a look of utter horror.

# CHAPTER 39

Danny had an emergency meeting in Paris that needed his personal attention.

"I'll go with you," Rose offered.

"You'd be bored. I'll be in meetings most of the time anyway."

"Obviously," Rose said, trying to keep the exasperation out of her voice. "I'm worried about Mary. We haven't heard from her in over two months."

"I'm sure she's busy with her studies. I'll call with an update."

Rose raised her eyebrows, nodding. "That's very thoughtful of you," she said, pleased that her husband was at least being accommodating.

They walked to the front door. Rose watched as Danny went down the front steps. He wore a pristine charcoal gray Ralf St. Lauren suit, white shirt, and what he fondly called his 'power red' silk tie. His freshly cut hair, and graying sideburns, made him all the more handsome to Rose. *Damn him,* she thought, as Danny slipped behind the wheel of his black Mercedes.

Despite all that had happened between them, Rose was still in love with Danny. She stood on the front deck watching him drive away, wondering for the millionth time how their relationship would have been had James not died. But, of course, she would never know.

Rose sighed, and went back inside *Hollyberry House*, thinking she would have the servants rearrange the furniture in the family room. Maybe she would even invite Iris and Betty for dinner. Yes. That's what she would do. That was a plan.

***

Jet lag had never been a problem for Danny, despite the fact he was older now. After they landed in Paris, he immediately went to the newly opened offices of Oxman & Sons, Inc. thrilled to have made the decision to grow the pharmaceutical business internationally.

The following afternoon, after several important meetings, Danny went to Mary's apartment. He thought about calling first, then changed his mind, deciding to surprise her instead.

The doorman Georgio, who had only seen Danny a few times in person, recognized him anyway. The man's photograph had been all over the French newspapers recently; the articles saying something about him moving his company to Paris.

"Good evening, Dr. Oxman," he said, furrowing his brow.

Danny nodded, waiting for Georgio to open the door, but Georgio, his hand on the oblong handle, hesitated. He liked Mary. He was also worried about her. She wasn't looking too good these last couple of months. He thought perhaps she didn't want her father to know or perhaps –

"Please. The door," Danny said, lifting his eyebrows.

"I don't think your daughter is home, sir," Georgio hedged, knowing full well she hadn't left the apartment in days.

"Then I'll wait for her inside," Danny quipped, annoyed.

Reluctantly, Georgio opened the door.

Danny took the elevator to Mary's floor, than let himself into her apartment. The moment he stepped inside a rancid smell took him aback while he quickly surveyed the scene. The place was in disarray with clothes scattered on the floor, and unwashed glasses, and dirtied dishes abandoned on table tops. He had no way of knowing that Mary had long ago dismissed the help to wallow in her self-pity.

Danny had come to surprise Mary; instead, he was the one surprised.

Before he had a chance to call out for her, Mary appeared, wearing a long black robe. At the sight of his daughter, he caught his breath.

"Mary! What in God's name is going on?" He cried.

Mary knew how bad she looked, and cringed. "I...think I overworked myself, daddy," she managed as he reached down to hug her. Mary melted against him, feeling like a child again safe in her father's arms; reveling in the musky scent of his familiar cologne.

Danny pulled back first, held Mary at arms-length, and did a quick inventory. Mary had felt skeletal against his body; her face was drawn, her eyes huge with black circles under them, her complexion deathly white.

"You need to go to hospital."

Mary started to protest, but she knew that was useless.

Nurses at St. Lucas took blood, and urine samples. They hydrated her with IV solution, and at Danny's insistence, freshly cooked meals from fine restaurants were delivered to her bedside. Mary was given vitamins, and warm towels, and whatever else she needed or asked for, except for her endless demands to be discharged.

"I'm twenty four years old," she argued. "I have rights."

But she knew whatever her argument, her father's influence was more powerful.

As promised, Danny phoned Rose.

"Oh my God, Danny. What's wrong with her?"

Although he had seen that Mary was suffering from severe depression, and self- neglect as a result, he had no definitive answer.

"At this point, I'm not certain," he told her.

"No idea? You're a *doctor*!" Rose said.

"I need to see the results of Mary's tests," Danny explained, hoping she heard him through her sobs.

"Is…is she going to, um, I mean is she going to…?"

And Danny, who knew what his wife was thinking, replied, "She's going to be fine, Rose. Don't worry."

And this time he would make sure to keep that promise.

# CHAPTER 40

As CEO of St. Lucas Hospital, Dr. Robert J. Thorton was made aware of Mary's admission the moment she arrived. Although he didn't know Danny personally from when he himself lived in the states, like everyone else in the building, he was well aware of the Oxman prestige; therefore, when Mary was admitted as a crisis patient, Dr. Thorton took a personal interest in her case.

"I'm sorry about your daughter's condition," he told Danny, skimming through her chart. "She's in pretty rough shape. Lucky you got her here when you did." His eyes fell upon a page. "How long has she been using?"

"Using? Using what?" Danny asked.

"The cocaine. The pills. The test results -

"There has to be some mistake," Danny replied, crossing his arms. "Mary would *never* use drugs."

*How could he not know?* Dr. Thorton wondered.

"Well, the test results indicate otherwise."

Danny started to protest, then stopped, realizing this man had no reason to lie.

"There's more," Dr. Thorton said, clearing his throat.

"Oh?"

"Mary is being treated for Syphilis."

Danny felt a frisson of unexpected relief. "Oh, well. That's easily taken care of," he said, waving a hand, as though they were talking about just any patient.

"And she's pregnant."

Silence then, "Pregnant?"

"I take it they haven't told you yet?"

"Who?"

Dr. Thorton had not heard that Mary had ever been married – surely that news would have had the media buzzing - so he said tactfully, "Mary and her, um husband. Has he been notified?"

And Danny heard himself say, "He's dead. Shortly after they were married."

"I'm sorry to hear that. It will be rough for Mary then to go it alone."

"Car accident. A tragedy really," Danny continued, his mind reeling. "And she won't be alone. I'm taking her back to the states."

"That would be in her best interest. She'll need to be here a week or so though, before she's strong enough to go with you." Dr. Thorton said, looking up from Mary's chart. He saw the anguish in Danny's face, and forced himself to forge ahead.

"Will your daughter consider an abortion? I mean, under the circumstances, I think…

"What? Why would she…Danny began and then realizing, "How far along is she?"

"The estimate is fourteen weeks. The drugs she has been using -

" - May *not* affect the fetus," Danny finished. "It's too soon in her pregnancy to make that prognosis."

Dr. Thorton frowned. "Of course, one never knows for *certain*, but the facts remain -

"Thank you for the information," Danny said, rising. "I appreciate you taking such a keen interest in my daughter's well-being. Mary will be fine. Her baby will be fine. She's going to give me a grandson."

Danny turned to leave, then turned back, gazing directly into Dr. Thorton's eyes. "I'm sure Mary's medical information will remain private, yes?"

"Of course."

"Good. That's good. I wouldn't want Mary's condition to get out in the media. I am certain you want the same."

"Absolutely."

When Danny left the office, Dr. Thorton buzzed his secretary.

"Ellen, I'm not taking any calls from reporters," he informed her in French. "As far as anyone here is concerned, there is no Mary Oxman being treated at St. Lucas as a patient. Make *sure* the hospital's PR department knows this."

With the receiver to her ear, Ellen watched Danny as he strode out of Dr. Thorton's office, straightening his tie. He gave her a cursory nod, and she swallowed, and said into the phone. "Oui, Dr. Thorton," as Danny walked out.

# CHAPTER 41

The following morning Danny pulled a chair up to Mary's bed, taking one of her hands in his. Her palm was clammy, her fingers birdlike, reminding him of his mother when she told him about her cancer diagnosis.

"What happened?" Danny asked, trying to mask his surprise, fear, and concern for his only child's health, and that of her unborn baby.

Mary was stunned when they told her she was pregnant. She was on the pill for God's sake. *Never* did she think…

"Mary?"

"I fell in love."

"Who is he?"

"Does it matter?"

"Did he leave you?"

Mary thought about the porn film she had unwittingly starred in.

"I left him," she lied. "He was no good. He was a mistake."

Which, at least, was partly true.

"Why the drugs?"

The pain in her father's eyes was unbearable, but at least he was trying to understand her position.

"It was a way for me to cope. You know, with my studies, my relationship troubles -

"Troubles? This man gave you trouble?" Danny bristled.

"Oh, well. *Not exactly.* You know, we just got into petty arguments, normal stuff," Mary emphasized. "But we were a good match overall."

She searched her mind for how to explain John Paul Chantel in a way her father would accept. "He had a bit of a roaming eye, but we were in the middle of trying to work things out when I decided my schooling was more important."

Danny did not believe her.

"Then why the cocaine? The pills?"

"Well, I started to experiment mostly to help me calm down, focus on my studies. I was using only since John…since we broke up. I swear."

*John. John who*? Danny wondered, but he filed the name away. There was always time to find out more about this man later, after the shock of what he was hearing wore off.

"When you're released Mary, I'm taking you back to *Hollyberry House*. You will have the baby at home."

"I don't want it."

"You say that now," Danny soothed. "You'll change your mind when you feel better."

The thought of being a mother nauseated Mary. "I don't want it," she repeated.

"You will have my grandson," Danny said, and Mary thought, *Over my dead body*.

But as usual, Danny had won. Mary flew home with him a few weeks later. Rose had refurbished Mary's old bedroom where she rested under close supervision. Danny had hired around the clock nurses to care for her, and Rose was so happy to have Mary home, that she hovered over her constantly.

"God mother, I don't have a terminal illness," Mary quipped. "Can I have some *space*?"

Rose tried to oblige, but it was difficult. She was thrilled at the thought of becoming a grandmother. Finally, she had a purpose in life. She would help raise the child, especially since Mary wasn't feeling well, all that maternal.

Rose spent her time knitting little sweaters, and hats for the baby, and now was able to join the conversations with her friends, who were already grandmothers reveling in their happiness for her good fortune.

"You'll *love* being a grandmother," Ethel gushed, and Rosemary said with a tilt of her head, "I didn't know Mary had married."

"It was a spur of the moment decision," Rose explained, then added, "He died in a car accident."

"How *terrible*."

"Awful."

"So *young*. So much to live for."

The only woman who didn't respond right away was Hazel, a skeptic at heart, and the town gossip. "When did all this happen? I didn't hear about Mary's wedding. Who did she marry? And when?"

Rose could see her mentally calculating the months. She blushed, looked away, then said, "I really don't want to go into it."

"I'm a bit insulted that there was a wedding, and we all were not invited," Hazel snipped, waving her hand in the general direction of the other women. "I think -

It was Rosemary who came to the rescue. Picking up her knitting needles she said, "Oh, Ethel. Who cares? Mary's husband *died* for heaven's sake." She turned to Rose, and said knowingly, "It really is okay, Rose. These things happen. Just yesterday I heard that Mindy Thomas's daughter was sleeping with –

And the conversation resumed.

***

The rest of that week, Rose concentrated on decorating the nursery. She hired house painters who transformed the room into soft hues of yellow, blue, and pink.

"The primary color will become prominent when we know if

you're having a boy or a girl," Rose told Mary, her hands furiously working her knitting needles. "Your father wants a grandson."

Mary blanched. "If I have a son maybe he'll turn out like James," she snapped.

Rose stiffened. Mary stared at her mother, not caring how she felt. Mary hated her mother, who had always loved James more than her, and who was also responsibility for her father's unhappiness. Her mother deserved to suffer.

"You mustn't think that way, Mary," Rose managed, and fled the room, leaving Mary in blessed peace.

Later, Rose broached the subject with Danny, but of course he had already considered the possibility. Besides, he was more concerned about the fact Mary had been using illicit drugs, information he decided to keep from Rose.

"There's a chance," he said. "But let's not go there unless we have to."

"If I remember correctly, boys are more likely to get Muscular Dystrophy than girls," Rose mused.

"Only a twenty-five percent chance," Danny said. "Besides it's 1985. Medical care has vastly changed. The chances are nil."

A month later, Danny discovered his calculation was wrong.

# CHAPTER 42

"Congratulations!" Dr. Gerry boomed. "You're having *twins*."

Mary was stunned into silence. Danny and Rose beamed. Danny even squeezed his wife's hand.

"How *wonderful!*" Rose said.

"Marvelous," Danny agreed.

They looked down at their daughter lying on the examination table, mistaking her facial expression of pure horror for disbelief.

"Don't worry, honey. You'll have plenty of help," Danny assured her, patting one arm.

"Boys or girls?" Rose asked.

Dr. Gerry smiled. "The way the babies are positioned makes it difficult to tell right now. We can do another ultrasound later, but of course they're not foolproof," he warned.

A nurse took a warm cloth, gently wiping gel from Mary's abdomen.

"She's having boys," Danny declared.

"But I must know for sure, Daniel," Rose told him, then turning to Dr. Gerry, winked and said, "I'm decorating the nursery."

"Ah, yes. The easy part."

"The *fun* part," Rose chuckled.

Mary listened to the conversation in complete misery. When the babies had first moved inside of her, she had felt like they were alien beings struggling to get out. And she wanted them out. The sooner, the better.

"What's her due date?" Rose asked.

"Mid-May if she goes full term."

*Five more months*! *I can't bear that,* Mary thought, and bent over the examination table, holding one hand over her slightly rounded abdomen, vomiting onto the floor.

"Morning sickness," Rose said, sympathetically rubbing Mary's back. "You'll be fine, dear."

Mary vomited again.

***

On March 28th, 1985 Mary went into labor at 1:22 a.m. Her first son was delivered at 5:10 a.m., and the second boy arrived three minutes later. Since the infants were premature, they were whisked away for medical treatment before Mary could cradle them.

"I'm sorry you weren't able to bond with the boys," Rose told Mary, patting her daughter's hand. "But there will be plenty of time for that later."

Mary blanched. Rose misunderstood her daughter's expression, and soothed, "I know darling, but you'll have these beautiful children forever. No worries."

When it came time to name the boys, Mary had no preferences, so Danny and Rose did the honor for her. The oldest they named Xavier, and his younger brother, Jack. They were identical twins.

The infants were brought to Mary's room five times a day, then whisked back to the nursery, which was Mary's favorite part of the visits.

"When will I get out of here?" Mary asked a nurse four days into her hospital stay, as the woman took Xavier from her arms. The woman tilted her head. "Any time you want."

"What?"

"Didn't the doctors tell you? You can leave the hospital whenever you wish. It's the babies who need to stay oh, another couple of weeks, I believe."

Mary fumed inside. It had to be her father who was keeping her in this prison!

"Dad. Can I go home?" Mary asked, the next time he and Rose came to visit.

"I thought it best you stay in the hospital, so you can be close to your babies instead of going back and forth from home," he explained. "Too exhausting. You'll need your strength when the twins get home."

*God, I'm stuck in this damn place because of these stupid kids*, Mary thought, but dared not share these feelings with her parents. They had no idea how much she despised having given birth. She had just turned twenty-five years old, and had always known motherhood was not for her.

Mary stayed in the hospital against her will for another three weeks, pretending to play the part of the attentive mother, while secretly plotting her revenge on John Paul Chantel. Of course, there was no way to reach him; tell him the news. Mary decided it was her duty to seek him out, and make him pay for getting her pregnant.

*And he will pay dearly*, she decided.

As Mary formulated her plans, Danny had ordered an assortment of tests for MS, and other genetic disorders; however, all the lab results came back normal. Danny and Rose breathed sighs of relief.

"Thank God," Danny said, and Rose said, "I would *die* if something was wrong with them. They are the most beautiful infants ever born."

This thinking may have been Danny and Rose's sentiments, but when Mary was home, and forced to interact with the boys, she viewed them as ugly little *things* with their red, wrinkled faces, half closed eyes, and little stick arms, and legs. They were annoying as hell too, always grabbing at her chest, hurting her tender breasts when she was forced to cradle them, not to mention the constant gurgling and spitting up on her clothing, usually on her best designer labels.

To please her father, Mary breast feed the infants even though she found no pleasure in that age-old practice.

"Breast milk is the best form of nutrition for infants," Danny assured her, and Rose added, "It helps with the bonding process."

Rose had read that, and other valuable information, in a new book a friend had given her authored by a Dr. Spock. It was a popular book that offered what Rose thought was tons of valuable updated information on how to care for infants; information that Rose wish she had known when she was raising her own children. Now she handed the thick paperback to Mary, who pretended to read it when her parents were around.

*** 

Luckily for Mary, her breast milk did not contain enough nutrients for little Xavier and Jack, so they were forced to switch to being bottle fed.

"That's too bad," Rose said, shaking her head, and Mary readily agreed. "Well, that's life," she sighed.

It was a few days later that Rose admitted to herself Mary was not adjusting well to motherhood. She barely looked at the infants, let alone changed diapers, or fed them. Instead, she spent most of her time out of the house with her old friends, or on the phone with them, ignoring her sons.

"I'm concerned about Mary," Rose confided in Danny. "She just doesn't seem interested in the well being of the children. It's strange. I feel like, well…like she wishes they were never born."

"I noticed that too," Danny said. "It could be postpartum depression."

"Perhaps, but it's not like she's moping around. Mary is out of the house more than she's home," Rose replied, to which Danny could not disagree. He wondered if she was using again, but there were no clear-cut signs of that, so he said, "Well, she's still young. Maybe she just needs time to adjust."

"Maybe," Rose said doubtfully. "I'll try and encourage her to be more attentive."

A cry rang out from the nursery. Rose jumped up to attend to the children.

# CHAPTER 43

When the boys turned six months old, Mary announced she was going back to Paris to try to work out her relationship with their father.

"Who is he?" Danny asked, searching for his cufflinks that he was sure he left on a side table, hoping he sounded nonchalant. He thought about this John person Mary had mentioned at St. Lucas back in France.

"I'll tell you if he comes around to the idea of being part of this family," Mary said evasively. "I promise. Do you mind taking care of the boys until I return?"

Since Xavier and Jack were born, Mary refused to call them by their given names. It was always the 'boys' or 'kids' or "babies."

"Of course we will, darling," Rose said. "They are the cutest little things, Mary. Just the other day Xavier started to creep around -

"Thanks. I appreciate all your help," Mary said, and went to pack her things.

Rose and Danny saw their daughter off at the airport a week later, then settled into a routine. Danny went back to work, and Rose back home, but this time with a light heart.

*I finally have a purpose in life,* she thought. *I must pour all my energy into raising these children while Mary is away.*

From the start, Xavier and Jack were an absolute delight. They also brought Danny and Rose closer together. At least they had their grandchildren to talk about when Danny came home for dinner, which was most nights now, since the boys were there waiting for him.

"Aren't they adorable?" Rose gushed, watching the now one-year old twins play with toys in the nursery they shared. They were mirror images of each other, and so, at least for Danny, difficult to tell apart.

"Xavier?" He asked, plucking one of his grandsons from the blue carpet.

"No. Jack."

"How can you tell?"

Rose shrugged. "It's a woman thing, I guess."

At Ethel's suggestion, Rose had tiny bracelets made with each of the twin's names on them just for Danny.

"That's much better," Danny said, and he smiled at Rose in such a way as to make her feel that perhaps her husband did love her after all.

*She's not such a bad wife*, Danny thought, watching Rose fussing over their grandchildren. *I must be getting soft in my old age.*

And it was true. Ronnie was only a distant memory now.

Mary called three months after she had gone back to Paris to tell them she was now living with the father of the twins. Danny and Rose wanted to meet the man, but Mary made excuses as to why the time wasn't right. After several attempts, they gave up. The reality was that Mary was still searching for John Paul Chantel; searching to seek her revenge.

"I hate to see Mary absent from her children's lives," Rose frowned, and Danny agreed, but there was nothing they could do to persuade her to return home.

# CHAPTER 44

As the boys grew older, they seemed to morph into one physical being with the same facial expression, and body types; even their voices were difficult to tell apart. Both had dark hair like the Oxman side of the family, and light gray eyes like the Kennedy's. They also had some mannerisms that reminded Danny and Rose of Mary, but that's where the similarities ended between the boys and their mother.

Over the next few years it became apparent that Xavier was the more intelligent of the two. He was the first to eat, walk, and talk. He was the first to learn how to stack toy blocks, use the toilet; catch a plastic ball, and learn the rules of simple board games. Xavier was bright, and witty, and funny. He loved attention, and usually got it from everyone.

On the contrary, Jack was quiet, timid, and serious; content to let his brother enjoy the limelight. Jack adored Xavier. He shared his toys, and food with him, and followed his brother around the house like a puppy.

From the start of elementary school, Danny and Rose discovered that Xavier was a fast learner, while Jack was a day dreamer, and had trouble keeping up with his school work. Rose noticed that Xavier tried to help his more socially awkward brother fit in with the other children, which pleased her no end.

One day when the twins were in sixth grade, the Headmaster of *Steward School for Boys* phoned Rose.

"Xavier got into some trouble today," Phillip Albertson told her.

"Xavier?" Rose chuckled. "Oh no, I'm sure you have the wrong child. Xavier would *never* hurt –

"Oh, but he did," Mr. Albertson said. "Xavier got into a fist fight in the gymnasium with another boy, who suffered a severely blackened eye. The academy nurse is tending to him now."

"*Xavier* did - ? No, no. That's impossible –

"Hold on a moment," Mr. Albertson said. After a bit of rustling, Rose heard Xavier's voice on the other end.

"It's true, grandma. I did get into a fight. But I had to! I…I had *no choice*."

"I see," Rose said, perplexed. "Well. We'll discuss your part in this later. Put Mr. Albertson back on the line, please."

"Tell me what happened?" Rose asked, and he did. As the man's words formed sentences, and the sentences told the story, Rose felt an unexpected moment of pride.

When Danny and Rose confronted Xavier that evening, he looked them right in their eyes and said, "Bryan Adams deserved all he got! He was making fun of Jack. He called him a *weirdo*. A *psycho* in front of the entire volleyball team!"

Danny's mind went back in time to when he had been beaten by Simon Coots and his gang, and he piped up with, "I understand. You did the right thing, Xavier."

Although Rose secretly agreed with her husband she said, with a hand on one hip, "Violence is never the answer to a problem," to which Danny replied, "Maybe not for you, Rose." He turned towards Xavier repeating, "You did the right thing," then as was his habit, Danny turned and walked away.

Rose and Xavier watched him leave.

"Jack is lucky to have you," Rose told her grandson. "But don't let something like this happen again, *please.* There are more appropriate ways to handle these types of situations."

"Yes, grandma," Xavier said. "I wish I could do more to help Jack, though. He really doesn't fit in with the other kids." He paused, not wanting to upset his grandmother further, but blurted out,

"If only our mother was here, she could probably –

"Shhhhh," Rose comforted. "Your mother loves you. She's just unable to show –

"*Love us*?" Xavier laughed, and the sarcasm in his voice startled Rose. "She doesn't even *know* us."

Rose had no argument there.

"Well, I suppose. You may have a point. I guess...Rose began, then steered the conversation in another direction. Hey, do you and Jack want to go to a movie tonight? I'll take a look in the newspaper to see what's playing."

Xavier watched his grandmother leave the family room, and sighed, upset that he had upset her. But what was he to do? The boys at school were always making fun of Jack, and the girls laughed when they thought Jack couldn't hear them. Maybe the reaction of the other kids didn't seem to bother Jack, but Xavier was livid at their insensitivity.

# CHAPTER 45

The years flew by, and finally during the early 1990's, the twins hit puberty, both fine looking young men. As Danny observed both of his grandson's personalities emerge in young adulthood, he decided that it was Xavier who would take over Oxman & Sons, Inc. As for Jack…well, Danny felt his other grandson would make a fine vice president of one of the divisions, with Xavier overseeing his work.

Meanwhile, Mary was still living in France, telling her parents that she was in an on again off again relationship with the twin's father. She had visited the states a handful of times, and Danny and Rose did their best to travel to France with the boys a few times a year so they could visit with her, hoping that during one of these visits they would finally meet this John person Mary referred to, but without luck. He was never at her apartment when they arrived, and Mary had an army of excuses why not. As for the actual visits with Mary, they were awkward, at best. While Jack seemed content to be with his mother, Xavier not so much; he was always relieved when it was time to go home, while Jack clung to Mary not wanting to leave her.

For their part, Danny and Rose knew little about Mary's life abroad even though they consistently inquired. They knew she was living off her trust fund, but that was about it. Danny was fine with the money Mary used to support herself simply because she appeared healthy.

As for the boys, they were polite to Mary when they did see her. They knew she was their mother, but that was about it. Only Jack kept one old photograph of her on his night table, and was the only one to ask questions about why Mary did not live with them, and who their father was. Danny and Rose made vague excuses, and explanations, until finally he grew tired of asking.

"It's actually good the father isn't involved," Rose said philosophically on their private jet back to the states after one visit.

"Oh. How's that?" Danny asked.

"Well, if this man was interested in Mary, and the well being of the boys, he may decide he wants them to go live in France –

"Over my dead body," Danny quipped, and Rose had no reason to pick up on the absolute truth that was that statement.

***

One night soon after the boys had just celebrated their fourteenth birthday, Danny overheard Jack talking to someone in his bedroom. The twins each had their own room on the third floor now, because Danny thought they needed personal space.

*Was Jack with a friend? Rose had not mentioned anything about a sleepover.* Danny went to check.

He discovered Jack snuggled under the covers propped up on pillows, holding the edges of a paperback book in both hands.

"Oh, you're reading," Danny said, feeling a strange sort of relief.

"My English teacher says reading aloud helps you concentrate better," he said. "Did I disturb you?"

"Not at all," Danny assured him. "I thought you had a friend over, that's all."

"No. Just me. Good night Grandpa."

"Good night."

Jack went back to his book.

A week later, Danny and Rose came home late from a dinner party.

"How did the kids make out, Gretchen?" Danny asked the nanny.

"Oh, they watched a movie, played a card game together, then fell asleep early. As usual, no trouble. No trouble at all."

Rose went to check on Xavier, and Danny peered inside at

Jack lying on his back in his bed, fast asleep, breathing evenly. A nightlight glowed softly against one wall. Satisfied, Danny closed the door with a soft click.

Immediately, Jack opened his eyes, stared at the ceiling for a moment, and then turned his head.

From a corner of the bedroom a voice whispered, *Your grandfather is gone. Come here Jack. Come sit with me.*

Jack threw off the covers, and got out of bed, giggling. He opened a window, then the screen, and put one leg over the window sill, then the other, balancing on his buttocks, the soles of his bare feet flat against the siding of the house, while his left hand held onto the frame.

Jack titled his chin upwards. A soft wind blew cooling his face. He smelled the sweet summer scents of his grandparents' garden, the aroma of the rose beds, and honeysuckle bushes far below. A full moon hung in a clear, star speckled sky. His friend came and sat beside him and said, *Follow me Jack. We can fly if we want to. Like Peter Pan. Come on!*

# CHAPTER 46

Jack, precariously balancing on the window ledge, felt like he and Harry *could* fly, right to the moon and back, if they wanted to. It was an exhilarating feeling of absolute freedom.

Jack looked at Harry, marveling at how much his new friend was so much like Xavier – confident, adventurous, and not afraid to try new things, unlike Jack. Harry's voice was clear as a bell, deep, like a man's, but Jack knew he was exactly his own age, because they shared the same birthday. He lived in the shed near the garage.

*Don't tell anyone about me, Jack,* Harry had repeatedly warned him. *They'll make me go away.*

Harry was Jack's only real friend; the only person who truly understood him, even more than Xavier. The kids Jack knew at school were mean to him. Most of them smoked pot, and made fun of Jack because he wasn't into experimenting with drugs, or having sex with random girls.

On the other hand, Xavier loved to party. Sometimes he convinced Jack to go out with him, wanting his little brother to fit in. Xavier instinctively knew that Jack was 'different.' Sometimes Jack went to the parties just to make his brother happy. If anyone gave Jack a hard time ,though, Xavier shot them down.

"Your brother is like totally *bonkers*, Xavier. He talks to himself. He's *Nuts*."

"Leave him alone, Alfred. At least he's not *gay* like you."

"How do you – Alfred started then turned and fled.

But Xavier knew that Alfred had a point. So as not to worry his grandmother, he approached Danny instead.

"I'm concerned about Jack," he told him.

"In what way?"

Xavier thought a moment. "It's hard to explain."

"The talking to himself? The always seeming to be distracted?"

Xavier sighed with relief. "You notice too then."

"Yes," Danny said. "I most definitely do."

"I just don't get Jack sometimes. I see him at the caf at school. He doesn't talk to the other kids. Mostly he just mutters while he eats. The kids make fun of him."

Danny's eyes darkened as he remembered hanging Simon Coots cat from a rusted basketball hoop during his own childhood, and Xavier was quick to add, "Don't worry, grandpa. I always take care of him."

Danny grabbed Xavier's upper arms, and squeezed. "As you should," he said. "I don't want you to worry, though Xavier. I'll take care of Jack."

Xavier let out his breath. He knew his grandfather was a powerful man. If anyone could help his brother, it would be him.

"I want to get Jack tested," Danny told Rose the next day.

"Whatever for?"

"He spends too much time by himself."

Rose smiled. "Oh, that's just Jack. He loves to read, and hang out in the house with his books. That's what he *does*."

Danny thought about the differences between his grandsons. Xavier played basketball, and tennis, and enjoyed school trips, and swimming, and boating. He had a ton of friends too. Jack was a homebody, with no friends, and apparently no desire to make any.

"I think it would be a good idea for Jack to be tested," Danny repeated.

Rose felt a stab of alarm. The last time Danny had expressed this much concern was when he noticed problems with James.

"Jack doesn't have MS. He was tested for that," Rose began, but Danny cut her off.

"It's his mental health I'm concerned about," he said.

# CHAPTER 47

Danny arranged for a battery of psychological testing for Jack. When the results came in, the boy's Pediatrician, Dr. Carnes, was able to allay Danny's fears.

"Jack is fine. He's just overshadowed by his brother. It's not unusual for twins to look the same, yet possess different, sometimes even opposite, personality traits," he assured the Oxmans. "But, of course, you already know that, Danny."

Dr. Carnes studied the chart on his desk. "Jack is the more creative of the two, that's for sure. Leave him be. He'll come into his own when he's ready."

"Oh, that's wonderful news," Rose said, patting her graying hair against a palm. The Oxmans got up to leave when Danny unexpectedly turned to his wife and said, "Can I have a minute alone?"

Rose hesitated. "I suppose," she said. "Is there something I should know about?"

"Nothing serious. I'll meet you in the car in a few minutes."

Rose nodded, picked up the cane she had been depending on lately, thanked Dr. Carnes, and left.

"What's up?" Ethan asked.

Danny hesitated, then forced the words out.

"If the boy's mother –

"Mary."

"Yes, Mary. If Mary was on medication when she was pregnant, early on, I mean, and then stopped, could that medication in some way have harmed the fetus's development, resulting in psychological problems later on in life?"

Ethan leaned back in his chair, twirling the ends of the pen between his index finger tips and thumbs. "That depends. What was she taking?"

Danny hesitated.

The other man sighed. "What was she taking?" He repeated, placing the pen on the desk top.

Danny felt a vulnerability flow through his body, a feeling of weakness, which he despised. It was an alien, ugly, out-of-control feeling. "Cocaine, uppers, downers."

Ethan nodded. Nothing surprised him these days. "I see. For how long?"

Danny had no idea, but he knew she was over two months pregnant when he took her back to the states, so he said, "Early on in her pregnancy, but then she stopped. I made sure of that," he added for emphasis.

Ethan sighed. He was one of the few people who knew the boys were born out of wedlock, but he had not been privy about Mary's drug use. No one was. Danny had made certain that information stayed out of her medical records.

"Sometimes premmies, especially twins, will have learning disabilities as they develop, but I don't believe any drug use on Mary's part affected Jack's development, if as you say, she stopped in her first trimester, or we would have found evidence of a problem long ago. Truth is, Jack has a high IQ. Bordering on genius," Dr. Carnes assured him.

"But there's a chance Jack *could* have been psychologically harmed in some way because of…Danny could not bring himself to finish.

Dr. Carnes mimicked Dr. Thorton back at St. Lucas Hospital. "There's always a chance. But like I said, I highly doubt it at this point. Get the boy involved in some outside, or school activities. He's just shy. What's he interested in?"

And that was the problem.

"Nothing. We introduced him to all kinds of activities," Danny said, racking a hand through his hair. "Sometimes he takes a stab at getting involved in, let's say, a sport like tennis, but eventually he quits."

"Then force his hand."

Danny took that advice. He insisted Jack take up swimming, so Jack reluctantly joined Xavier's team at school. And then one day, out of the clear blue, Jack asked if he could take horseback riding lessons. He had watched an old western movie on television with Harry, and Harry said he thought horseback riding would be fun.

"Of course you can," Danny told him, pleased his grandson was finally showing interest in an activity that Xavier wanted nothing to do with.

"See? He's coming into his own," Rose said, smiling. "Just like Dr. Carnes predicted."

Danny bought Jack a feisty gelding that was boarded at a nearby riding facility called *Pleasant View Farms*. Jack loved the smell of fresh hay, the open fields, the corrals, and the natural smells in the barn. The first time he had successfully saddled his horse, and was about to mount though, he hesitated.

"What's wrong?"

Jack turned, and saw a girl about his age, studying him. She wore a black riding helmet with red hair streaming out from under it, and she had green eyes, and freckles, and a dimple smack in the middle of her chin. She held the reigns of a brown and white Palomino.

"I never rode a horse without an instructor nearby," Jack said.

The girl smiled, revealing silver braces. "Oh. Don't worry. You'll be fine. Who's your instructor?"

"Mr. Blackmore.'

"That's great! Mr. Blackmore was my first instructor too. You'll get the hang of riding." She studied his horse. "You have a beautiful gelding. What's his name?"

"*Slick*. What's yours?" Jack asked.

"*Rusty*."

Jack blushed. "I mean *your* name," he said.

The girl laughed, and the sound was like angels chuckling in heaven.

"Brie."

*God, she's beautiful,* Jack thought.

"Jack!" A voice called. He turned. Mr. Blackmore was motioning him over to the other side of the corral.

"I gotta go," Jack said, turning to leave.

Brie was smiling at him, and Jack felt an unfamiliar, yet pleasant stirring, in his groin.

"You'll do fine," she said, turning and waving. "See you around."

# CHAPTER 48

Over those summer months, Jack and Brie hung out at the stables caring for their horses, and riding along trails together when they weren't taking lessons. They enjoyed picnic lunches in the fields behind the stables, and took long lazy walks with each other at *Pleasant View Farms*, which had hundreds of acres of trails along mountainsides, valleys, and woods. Jack knew he was falling in love, and he felt that Brie was too, although he never said that he loved her aloud. He was waiting for the right time.

One crisp fall day, Jack saddled *Slick* and went for a trail ride by himself, since Brie wasn't around. It was a sunny day in late October, and he wished Brie was with him, but he enjoyed sitting in the saddle as *Slick* trotted along the dirt path. The maple trees were just starting to turn into beautiful shades of red, yellow, and orange. Jack saw a blue jay whiz past him just as he came upon an unexpected clearing, where he thought he spotted someone. *Slick* snorted. Jack pulled back on the reigns, and the horse stopped. Staring straight ahead, Jack caught his breath at what he saw.

One of the stable hands, Timothy Stapleton, and Brie were standing in the clearing, talking softly to each other. They were standing close together. Timothy put a hand to her cheek, and Jack saw Brie smile up at him. His heart stopped. Brie moved in closer, and he thought Timothy was going to kiss her. Jack couldn't bear to watch. He turned *Slick* around, hitting the gelding's sides. The horse galloped back towards the stable with Jack heartsick at what he had just witnessed.

When Jack arrived home later that afternoon Harry said, *I think he likes her.*

"Who?"

*You know who. That Timothy guy. He's always looking at Brie's breasts. She's a beautiful girl.*

"No, Harry," Jack said." I mean, yes Brie *is* really beautiful, but she's not interested in that Timothy jerk."

*Pay attention, Jack! I think Brie likes you now, but…*

"But what?"

*That could easily change. Let's face it. Tim's blonde. Girls love blonde, handsome men. He's tall. Better looking than you too. Have you seen his muscles? I think -*

"Stop it!" Jack snapped. He picked up a glass, smashing it on the granite countertop, the broken pieces slicing the fingers of his left hand.

"*Shit*! Now look what you made me do, Harry!" Jack snapped, rinsing the blood in the kitchen sink, a rage building up inside of him.

"What happened?" Rose said, coming into the kitchen. "Oh my God, Jack! You're bleeding."

"I'm fine."

Rose left, and returned shortly after, holding a bottle of peroxide, and a bandage. Jack let her tend to his hand.

"Sorry grandma. It was an accident," Jack said.

As Rose worked, she said casually. "Were you talking to someone? I thought I heard you say something when I came into the room."

"I just got off the phone with my friend, Harry," Jack said, nodding towards a wall phone.

Rose started to ask if he had argued with this Harry person, but decided against it. The boy was allowed some privacy.

"Rose, gently patting the sticky edges of the bandage around the wound exclaimed, "All set. Good to go," then started recapping the dark brown Peroxide bottle. "I'll have your grandfather take a look at that cut later. We don't want it to get infected."

Both Jack and Harry nodded in unison, then they turned, and walked out of the room, side by side.

# CHAPTER 49

The following day, Jack and Brie were together, grooming their horses just outside the main barn. Pumpkins and yellow squash were piled in wagons about the grounds, and stalks of golden hay were leaning up against the sides of barn doors as decorations. The day was crisp and cool.

"I don't like that Timothy guy," Jack blurted out.

"Who?" Brie asked.

Jack pointed towards Timothy Stapleton, who stood at the other end of the barn. Timothy saw him, then averted his eyes, sticking a shovel under a pile of horse manure. There were many occasions when Timothy stared at Jack when he thought Jack was unaware.

Now Brie said. "Timothy? Oh, he's okay. Just a big flirt."

"What do you mean?" Jack said, thinking about the way Timothy had cupped Brie's face in his hand the day before.

"Oh, well. He's asked me out a few times," Brie said, waving her hand dismissively. "But he's older than me. My father would *never* allow me to date a 19 year old."

Jack found himself saying, "What would he feel about a 16 year old?"

Brie tilted her head up, smiling. "Are you officially asking me out Jack Oxman?" She asked.

Jack blushed, berating himself inwardly. "Well, I just thought it would nice to, like… I don't know… to be, well… a couple."

"I'd like that," Brie said, lifting her eyebrows. "It's official then. I was waiting for you to ask me out ever since we first met, silly.

That's why I keep telling Timothy to leave me alone."

Jack's face darkened. Brie must have seen the look in his eyes, because she put a hand on his arm, sending shivers of pleasure straight up to this heart.

"I'd take you over that old Timothy Stapleton any day," Brie said. "Now, come on. Let's go for a ride."

Jack mounted his horse; Brie mounted hers, and off they went, riding side by side in one of the smaller corrals, laughing, then Brie kicked *Rusty* into a gallop, racing ahead of Jack, who leaned forward in his saddle, kicking *Slick's* sides, urging his horse into a gallop too.

"You won't win this race, Brie!" Jack shouted.

From the other side of the fencing, Timothy watched, frowning.

*Bite me*, Jack thought, and laughed aloud.

***

Danny was in his study when Jack walked by in the hallway.

"Jack. Can I see you a moment?"

"Sure, grandpa. What's up?"

"Have a seat."

When grandpa said, "Have a seat," it was usually serious. Jack sat.

"Who's this Harry person you talk to?"

"Who?"

"That's what I'm asking."

Jack's mind was racing. "Oh, Harry. Yeah, well, he's just a friend I met at school."

Danny studied his grandson, looking for signs of deceit, but found none.

Satisfied, he said, "What's his last name?"

"His…last name?" Jack shrugged, as if not knowing was no big deal. "I forgot."

"According to Xavier, and your grandmother, you've been talking to him by phone a lot lately. Would you like to have him over for a visit?"

"Um," Jack tilted his head. Harry whispered, *Say yes.*

"Yes."

"Wonderful." Danny opened his day planner. "I'd like to meet this young man. Ask him if next Friday is okay. Maybe you two can go to a movie."

Harry whispered, *Say fine.*

"Fine," Jack said, nodding.

When the time came for Harry to visit though, Jack told his grandparents he was sick with the flu.

"Well, it is turning into a chilly fall," Rose said, looking over at Danny.

Danny suggested another day, but again Harry was a no show.

"He said he has some family issues," Jack explained.

His grandparents, and Xavier, just looked at him, then Xavier and Danny went off for a Sunday morning ride in Danny's new Porsche.

"I don't think there *is* a Harry," Xavier said, shaking his head.

"Maybe on the swim team?" Danny offered.

"I don't know anyone by that name, grandpa. I'm really worried about Jack," Xavier said.

So was Danny.

# CHAPTER 50

Danny called the headmaster of Baron Academy first thing that Monday morning. He was determined to get to the bottom of this Harry mystery once and for all.

"Dr. Oxman is on the phone, Mr. Edwards," Susan said, as her boss walked by her desk. "Line one."

"I wonder what he wants." He hadn't meant to say the words aloud, and Susan said, "I guess you're going to have to ask."

Ben strode into his office, closing the door behind him.

"Good morning Dr. Oxman. What is –

"Do you have a student by the name of Harry enrolled there?"

The question caught him off guard. "Harry? Harry who?"

"That's what I want to know."

"Well, off hand, I…I would have to check," Ben said. "We have over 500 hundred students here, you understand."

"Then check," Danny said. "You can call me on my direct line when you have an answer."

"Sure, Dr. Oxman," Ben replied, glancing at his desk calendar. "I have several back to back meetings today, but I can -

"You have until noon," Danny said, and hung up.

Ben stared at the phone. He buzzed Susan. "Get me the list of every student enrolled since September."

"Oh gosh. I would need like, a day or two to do that," she calculated.

He glanced at the clock. "You have four hours," he told her.

Minutes before noon, Ben called Danny back.

"We don't have any students by the name of Harry, or Harold. The closest is Hand*el* –

"No, that's not it," Danny said. "This student allegedly goes by Harry. I'm sure of it."

Ben dreaded his next words, but he took a deep breath , then said, "Well, we do have a Harry Silverman. But he's not a student," he added quickly. "He's...well, he's Jack's gym teacher."

It was May of 2000. Danny thought back to the early 90's when a catholic priest, Father James Porter, was arrested and jailed for molesting hundreds of boys over a thirty-year period. The heinous acts took place in parishes close to Boston in Southeastern Massachusetts. If such atrocities could happen under the auspices of the Catholic Church, the same horror could be happening in an upscale private school in the Back Bay in Boston just as easily.

"I want to meet with him."

"Of course, Dr. Oxman," Ben said, chewing his lower lip. He worried that if there was a problem with Harry Silverman the school's reputation would suffer horribly. He put that thought out of his mind, hoping for the best.

The meeting took place at seven a.m. the next morning.

Susan watched the three men walk into her boss's office. Harry Silverman had sweat across his brow. Susan had no idea what was going down, but it sure didn't look good.

"My grandson Jack tells me that you spend quite a bit of time with him, Mr. Silverman," Danny said, without fan fare. "What's that about?"

It was Harry Silverman's first year teaching, fresh out of college.

"I... have no idea what you're talking about, sir. I don't...I mean, I have Jack in class, yes, but quite frankly he's very quiet, doesn't say much, and his athletic abilities are...he was going to say 'weak at best,' but one look into Danny's eyes made him change his tactic, "are getting stronger every day, but really sir, I hardly know your grandson. He… doesn't say much. He may be a twin, but he's nothing like his brother, Xavier." He knew he was babbling, but was unable to stop.

Ben asked, "Shall we invite Jack into this meeting, Dr. Oxman?"

Danny studied Harry Silverman, his facial expressions, posture, and hand gestures. He was shifting in his seat, one eyelid twitching.

"No. There's no need to bring Jack into this," he decided.

Danny ordered a background check on Harry Silverman, discovering the man had been arrested for two DWI's. One more and he would be jailed. That's all Danny needed to know.

The following day, the entire student body was informed that Mr. Silverman had been transferred out of the district.

When Jack told Harry the news, he sighed with relief. *I told you never to speak of me to anyone Jack. Thank God they misunderstood. Here's what I want you to do…*

A few days later, Jack announced, "Harry says he wants to come visit, if that's okay."

Danny, Rose, and Xavier exchanged glances.

"Harry?" Danny said. "Did you find out his last name?"

Jack nodded. "Blake. Harry Blake. He goes to Parkson High School."

"I thought you said he went to *our* school," Xavier said, but thinking back now thought maybe he had been wrong about that.

"No. *Parkson.* I met him at one of our swim meets, Xavier. He was on the opposing team. I'm sure I told her that."

Danny looked at Jack then over at Xavier who shrugged. "It's a possibility," Xavier said.

Harry came to visit at *Hollyberry House* the following weekend. He had never been inside such a spectacular home.

"Wow! You have a great place," he said to Rose.

"Thank you, Harry," she said. "There's a ping pong table in the family room, or if you brought your swim suit, there's a heated indoor pool. If not, you can borrow one of Jack's."

"That sounds great."

The boys disappeared. Rose immediately phoned Danny.

"Harry seems like a nice kid," she reported.

Danny's relief was instantaneous.

After dinner, Jack stood at the front door where he handed Blake Mathesonan a clear plastic bag filled with an ounce of Xavier's best pot, knowing his brother wouldn't miss it. He had so much more hidden in his bedroom.

"I really appreciate this, Blake," Jack said. I hope -

"No problemo," Blake told him, taking the stash. "If you need me again, just call. I'll clear my schedule."

Blake Matheson left the house. Jack shut the door behind him, then went back into the kitchen.

"Harry seems like a really nice kid," Rose said, smiling her approval.

"I *tried* to tell you that," Jack said, rolling his eyes.

A teapot on the stove started to whistle. Harry sat on top of its lid, his hands cupped over his mouth whispering, *Good job Jack, my man. Good job, indeed.*

# CHAPTER 51

Mary spotted John Paul Chantel by pure chance. He was sitting alone at a corner table in a small café nestled in the beautiful town of Bern in Switzerland. Mary had flown over from Paris to meet up with an old college friend there, who was backpacking his way through Europe.

At first, Mary didn't recognize John Paul - after all it had been years since she had last seen him in France - but yes, she was sure the man she pinpointed was him.

"Mary? What's wrong?" Stephan asked, sipping foam from his beer mug.

"I just spotted an old friend," Mary said, rising.

John Paul pulled bills out of his wallet, counted, and placed a few on the table. A server came by, scooped up the money, and thanked him. He rewarded her with his winning smile. When he started towards the exit, Mary was afforded a bird's eye view of his face.

God, he was still a gorgeous specimen of a man; older now, but still handsome, although now in a more refined, rather than rugged way.

*That's what my money did for him*! Mary thought, annoyed, then she remembered the details of porn film she had allowed him to talk her into. God, she had been so *stupid,* yet she understood why she had so readily agreed. There was a magnetism to the man that gripped her even now, despite his betrayal of her.

Mary started to follow John Paul out into the street when Stephan called out, "Hey, Mary. Where ya going? You haven't finished your drink."

In the parking lot behind the stone building, John Paul got behind the wheel of a gold-colored Lamborghini, brand new by the looks of it. Mary hopped into her rented Mercedes, and followed him out onto the street, thinking about Adele; anxious to ask John Paul if she had strangled the young girl during the taping of that porn flick so many years before. The not knowing had always tormented her.

At the next traffic light, John Paul turned right. So did Mary. She followed him for miles out of Bern, and into the countryside to an upper-class neighborhood, where the houses were spaced far apart, impressive, boasting of money. The Swiss Alps, majestic in the background, were white tipped, and clearly visible.

Finally, John Paul pulled into a winding driveway of a sprawling three story home, set back a hundred feet from the road. A garage door automatically opened, while the Lamborghini idled, patiently waiting.

*A garage that he paid for with my trust money*, Mary fumed.

She pursed her lips, watching the Lamborghini pull into the garage, and then the door slowly whirred closed behind it. She waited a few minutes until a light appeared in a downstairs window.

Then she parked the Mercedes off the road on the other side of the street, killed the engine, got out of the driver's seat, and made a beeline towards the front door. A dog barked viciously in the distance; a cool wind blew. Mary rang the front door bell, which set off a calming, melodic sound. This was not how she envisioned meeting up with John Paul. She knew she was being impulsive, but she couldn't stop herself.

The door swung open and finally, after all these years of searching and waiting, she found herself face to face with her former lover.

John Paul's eyes momentarily widened, then his facial muscles visibly relaxed. Stereo music played in the background; a classical piece by the great Beethoven.

"Hello, John Paul."

"Mary."

They stared at each other.

"How did you find me?"

"Does it matter?"

Mary studied his face, looking for a resemblance between his features, and that of the twins he had fathered.

"Can I come in?" She asked, surprising herself with how calm she sounded.

"Of course," John Paul said, graciously nodding, before stepping aside.

The living room was tastefully decorated. Not in black and white, but in soft tones of grays, and shades of purple and greens, and there was plush furniture, and original paintings by important artists hung on the walls. There was a crystal vase filled with a dozen red roses on a coffee table with a little card stuck in the middle of the stems.

Inside the living room, John Paul flipped a wall switch, and a gas-fueled fire went *poof* inside a marble-edged fireplace.

"Why did you come, Mary? Our deal is done. Your money, by the way, has been well spent, as you can see." He waved an arm in the air.

So, he had stashed her money in a Swiss bank account. Untraceable. Of course he did. She should have realized.

Despite her insane anger that had haunted her over the years, the sight of John Paul melted her heart. It was like she was the puppet, and he the puppet master. Standing in the room so close to him made it difficult for Mary to breathe. She had almost forgotten that she wanted him dead.

"I came to tell you about your sons," she began, and John Paul said, "Ah, yes. The twins. Xavier and Jack. I have been reading about their antics in American newspapers. They are handsome young men. You should be proud of them."

"You know about the boys?" Mary said, aghast.

"Of course, Cheri. How are they?"

Mary hadn't seen them in over a year. "They are being well taken care of. Don't you want to meet them?"

"Not in the least. I have no interest in them."

Mary felt tightness seize her chest. "How can you *say* that? You're their *father*."

"Ah, but you are wrong, Mary. Those boys have nothing to do with me." John Paul studied the perfectly manicured fingernails of his left hand.

"Of course they do! They're your *sons*, your flesh and blood."

"Impossible," he said, and smiled his magnificent smile.

Mary crossed her arms. "How can you be so certain?"

"Because I am infertile. I had a vasectomy eons ago. In my field, I must be certain that women cannot bear my children. Bad for business, you see."

Mary's head began to whirl. This could not be happening!

"You're wrong," she hissed. "The twins *have* to be your sons! I did not sleep around after we met. I…I – she wanted to say, "Loved you," but refrained.

"Are you sure, Mary, that there was no one else?" John Paul sat on a velvety couch, crossing his legs, his hands clasped behind his head. "What do you remember of the night I disappeared? The night we were at the *Squealing Hog* with Malachi and Peppie? What happened *that* night, Mary? Who did you sleep with then?"

Her mind went back in time. She remembered the dark European café, Malachi and Peppie, the smell of raw fish; she remembered drinking a sweet tasting concoction, then vomiting, before passing out, only to awaken the next day naked, in her own bed.

Alone.

Totally alone.

Anyone could have taken advantage of her that night without her awareness. Anyone at all.

"*You bastard!*" Mary yelled, and before she could stop herself, she grabbed a fire place iron, and swung it at his head.

John Paul jumped up, grabbing the thick stick in mid-air, then easily pulled it out of her hands.

"*Slut!* That was a mistake. And it was a mistake to come here." The viciousness in his voice was like a physical blow.

A woman's voice called, "John Paul? Is everything -

Amelia St. Pierre strode into the room then, looking lovely in a white pant suit, and bright red lipstick. She was older, yes, but still beautiful. At the sight of Mary, she stood stock-still.

"What are you doing here?" Amelia demanded, looking over at John Paul, who had thrown the iron to the floor, then back at Mary, her eyes slits.

"She was just leaving," John Paul told her.

"You should not have come here," Amelia snapped.

John Paul grabbed Mary's arm, and pulled her towards the door, hurting her. Mary gave out a little scream, kicking out at him, but John Paul was too strong. "Amelia is right. You should not have come here. Now you will wish you did not," he declared.

Amelia strode over to them, then stood behind John Paul, peering over his shoulder at her.

"You made a terrible mistake finding us. Have you forgotten that you killed poor Adele? We have the scarf to prove it! The scarf with your fingerprints all over it!" And John Paul snapped, "The video too. With your face, and Adele's, clearly visible. Perhaps now that you found us, we should let your almighty parents know what you did!"

Mary felt a burning rage build inside her; anger directed more at herself. She had been impulsive coming here. She should have waited; taken time to think about a strategy before confronting

John Paul. She should have waited! Strangely, Amelia had been a surprise. Somehow, Mary never thought she and John Paul was a real couple.

Mary turned, and ran out of the house, racing to her car. She did not allow the tears to flow until she had driven away. But she was not finished with John Paul Chantel. Not yet. Mary promised herself that he would pay dearly for what he had done to her.

*He'll be sorry I found him after all these years*, Mary thought. *He will pay*!

# CHAPTER 52

Brie came into the barn for her riding lesson. Jack took one look at her, then dropped the grooming brush he held.

"Brie? What *happened* to you?

Brie looked at her hands. "I slammed into a door."

One of her eyes was practically swollen shut, and there was a white bandage near her temple, tinged with a whisper of maroon.

"I don't believe you! Tell me the *truth*!" Jack demanded.

"I can't."

"You *have* to!"

Brie started to back away,  but Jack stepped forward, taking ahold of her arm, stopping her from running away.

"Tell me."

Brie looked around. "It was Timothy," she whispered. "He...

Jack waited. "He *what*?"

"Raped me."

Jack felt an instantaneous rage. Sudden. Hot. In the center of his chest. He took a swift intake of breath. "He *what*?"

"*Shhhh*. You heard me. *Please*, Jack. Don't tell anyone. If my father finds out he will *kill me*!"

"*You*? This wasn't' *your* fault," Jack shouted, amazed that she would even have such a thought. A tear slid down one of Brie's freckled cheeks, and he gently wiped it away, so as not to hurt her.

"I'll kill him!"

"No, Jack. Leave him be!"

"He needs to pay," Jack said, and before Brie could respond added, "I love you, Brie. I will do anything to keep you safe."

***

The UPS man came while Rose was home late one afternoon. She buzzed him through the wrought iron gate.

"Good morning, Pete," she said.

"Mornin' Mrs. Oxman." Pete hopped out of the driver's seat, went around to the back on the brown truck, rooted around, then returned, balancing a package in one hand, while holding a pad attached with a pen, out to her in the other.

"Maybe it's from Mary," he said, then blushed. "I'm sorry. I wasn't snooping. I just saw the return address."

Rose smiled. "Not to worry." She signed the pad, then handed it back to him, exchanging it for the box.

"How *is* Mary?"

Rose sighed. "Last time she called, which was a while ago, she was doing okay."

"God, I remember her when she was a kid," Pete said.

Rose smiled. "She's not a kid anymore."

"Right. Time sure does fly. How are the twins?"

Rose thought about Xavier. He was recently named Football Captain at the boys' private high school, and was dating a nice young woman from a good family that she and Danny approved of. And Jack was enjoying his riding lessons these last few weeks, and seemed to be more social too. He talked about a girl he had met at *Pleasant View Farms*.

"They're both good. Thank you for asking."

"That's wonderful," Pete said, climbing back into the driver's seat. "Well, good day, ma'am." He flipped the key in the ignition, then drove the truck around the circular driveway, and out the gate, which closed behind him.

Rose went back inside the house then, thinking it strange that Mary would send a package. She had never written a letter in all the years she was living in France, let alone sent anything via UPS. But Pete was right. The return address was from a sender in France. Curious, Rose found a pair of scissors in the den, then glanced at the label. The package was addressed to Danny. She hesitated. Although she was more than curious about the contents, she also thought it appropriate that Danny open it. Perhaps Mary wanted her father to have something special.

Rose sighed, placed the scissors back inside the drawer, and put the box on Danny's office desk at the same instant the phone rang.

"Rose, I need you to listen to me, and remain calm. Don't panic," Danny's voice rang out.

Rose panicked.

"What is it?" She cried, a hand moving to her throat, and when the story started to unfold, she felt her whole world crashing in around her.

Danny's whole world had crashed in all around him a half hour earlier. This after Inga burst into his inner office without knocking.

Dr. Oxman? There's a police detective here to see you," she said, wringing her hands. "Hanly. Detective Handley. I mean *Hanly*, I think."

Danny glanced at the wall clock. He had a board meeting to attend, and had wanted to rest a bit beforehand.

"If it's about a donation tell him…"

"It's not," Inga said. "It's about Jack."

# CHAPTER 53

Jack waited until late afternoon while the stable hands were getting the grounds ready for the next day. Most of the hired help had gone, save for Timothy and Clark. They were cleaning out stalls; putting away riding gear.

Jack strode over to Clark when he had distanced himself from Timothy.

"Why don't you head out? I'll help Timothy close up shop."

"I don't think my boss would like that." Clark frowned.

Jack handed him a one hundred dollar bill. "He doesn't have to know."

Clark licked his lips, his mind racing, then decided if the rich kid wanted to shovel horse shit who was he to argue?

"Sure, why not," he said, snatching the bill from Jack's hand.

Jack watched as Clark began to stuff his personal belongings into a backpack, feeling a cool breeze against his face as the sun began to set. Then slowly he pulled the zipper of his black sweatshirt upward, before turning full around.

*Now Jack*, Harry said, pointing.

Jack spotted a pitch fork leaning against a wall, and gripped the thick wooden handle in both hands. He heard the horses rooting for hay in their stalls, snorting. The smell of manure hung thick in the air. Jack glanced back at Clark, watching as he swung the strap of his back pack around one shoulder, and started out of the barn, then Jack turned, zeroing his attention on Timothy, who sat on a hay bail at the other end, smoking a cigarette, which of course, was against the rules.

*The Bastard! The kid thinks he's above the law*, Jack thought. *Well, not for long.*

As Timothy blew little circles of bluish smoke into the air, Brie strolled inside stopping just a few feet away from Timothy, who looked up, and that's when he noticed Jack standing rigid just two hundred feet away, holding a pitchfork, his eyes staring at him, blankly.

*"No, Jack!"* Brie screamed. *"Noooo!"*

And that's when Jack charged.

Timothy was blindsided. He saw Jack rushing towards him with the tongs of the pitchfork raised above his head, eyes wild.

*"What the fuck!"* He screamed.

*"You raped Brie. You gotta pay for that you bastard."*

Momentary confusion, and then Timothy held both hands over his head. Seconds later he felt the flat side of the prongs slam into both forearms as he stepped back; the force of the thick metal sending shooting pain throughout his body. Timothy screamed as he tripped, falling onto his back. Jack thrust the pitchfork downwards, intending to plunge the tines into Timothy's stomach, but Timothy rolled, and the tines struck the wooden floor with a screeching sound as they scraped against the planks. Jack raised the pitchfork again, and rammed it towards Timothy's chest, but by that time Timothy had started to push himself upwards, and the metal sank into one arm. A rain of blood spurted forth, and Timothy screamed, scrabbling to his feet. He managed to grab a black riding crop from a hook on the wall, whipping it through the air in front of Jack, but Jack was unperturbed, his heart pumping wildly as he thrust the pitchfork towards Timothy's chest again. Timothy stumbled backwards. This time the metal tines sank into his lower left leg.

It was then that Brie charged at Jack knocking him to the blood covered floor screaming, *"Stop! Right now. Jack! What's the matter with you?"*

As Jack strained to get away from her, the horses imprisoned in their stalls neighed wildly; their hoofs causing a cacophony of sound as they drummed them against the walls.

Jack found that Brie was surprisingly strong for a girl as she ripped the pitchfork from his clenched hands, then pinned his arms to his sides. He looked up into her eyes yelling, "*He has to pay for what he did to you, Brie. I want to kill the bastard for what he did!!*

Clark continued to hold Jack down, his face sweaty, gasping. "*Holy Christ Jack. Stop! What the fuck!?*"

# CHAPTER 54

*Cliff Manor Psychiatric Hospital* is located in Newport, Rhode Island. The dozen three story, red brick buildings are strategically placed on expansive well-tended lawns that branch off into pathways that lead to the ocean. When tourists drive by the impeccable grounds their first impression is that the facility is a five-star luxury resort way, out of their price ranges.

In reality, the locals know that *Cliff Manor Psychiatric Hospital* is reserved for the criminally insane.

Jack was seated in the office of Dr. Kathleen Politzer, a woman who had been practicing psychiatric medicine for over thirty years. Her desk was positioned near the door, so if patients were to make threatening moves, she would be the first to bolt.

Jack was seated near the back window, which was covered with thin checkered iron mesh, not discernable from the grounds outside. Dr. Politzer could not help feeling sorry for this particular patient. He came from a privileged background; his future looked bright, that is, before he tried to commit murder. And now, here he was - committed at *Cliff Manor* for God knew how long.

Harry floated in a corner of the room, peering down at Jack, unusually quiet.

"How are you feeling, Jack? Do you think the medication is working?"

"Doan know."

"Well, we did increase the dosages. It may take some time for the combination to absorb into your system. Have you heard from Brie lately? Has she come to visit?"

Harry whispered, *Say no.*

"No," Jack said.

Dr. Politzer studied his face. "She doesn't come during the night?"

*Say… of course… She isn't -*

Jack had trouble hearing Harry, but he mumbled, "'Course not. She doesn't…she isn't real."

Dr. Politzer nodded, then made a note in his chart. "And Harry? How about him?"

"Harry is… he's jus' a voice. Someone in my head," Jack said, mimicking what the other doctors had been hammering into his brain for the last week. "He's… not a person."

Harry folded his arms, frowning, but said nothing. Brie flew in through the barred window.

Dr. Politzer noticed Jack close the fingers of his right hand. She jotted another note.

"Do you remember attacking Timothy Stapleton?"

Despite the medication, Jack tensed. He started to say, *I want to kill him*, but said, "Yes," instead. The word came out, 'Yez."

"You remember that other stable hand," Dr. Politzer referred to Jack's chart. "Clark Barret stopping you?"

Jack knew it had been Brie that pinned him to the floor, begging him to stop his brutal attack on the bastard, but if that's what this woman wanted to hear…he nodded.

"You realize it's wrong to try to hurt another human being, don't you Jack?"

Brie whispered something unintelligible into his left ear. Jack tilted his head.

"Yeah."

"Yes, you know the attack was wrong?"

Jack thought Dr. Politzer was wrong, but something in the recesses of his brain made his say, "Uh huh."

"Timothy was badly maimed in that attack. His right forearm had to be amputated, and his leg is badly mangled. He may never walk again because of the injuries you inflicted upon him. How does that make you feel?" Dr. Politzer asked, searching Jack's face for signs of remorse. There was none.

Harry started to whisper loudly, interrupting Brie, which angered Jack. He wanted to know what she was trying to tell him.

Dr. Politzer wasn't sure the medications she prescribed were working as well as she had hoped, but initially prescribing any psychotropic drug was a hit and miss venture to start. She had long since decided her recommendation to the courts would be that Jack Oxman was mentally unsound at the time he attacked Timothy Stapleton. Being a minor, and with the defense team the Oxman family had put together, meant there was a good chance Jack would not be incarcerated anyway, not that she felt any schizophrenic should be. She would recommend long-term hospital care until they could figure out which medications worked best, and hoped that the intensive counseling sessions Jack was undergoing would help him back to reality.

Jack, unable to decipher what Brie was saying, let his forearms fall limply across his lap. "I doan wanna talk no more," he said. "I'm tired."

Dr. Politzer nodded, getting to her feet. "No problem. You can go back to your room now." She opened her office door, calling over a male orderly who accompanied Jack out of her office. Unbeknownst to her, Jack stepped out into the hallway only after he was certain that Harry and Brie were following him.

# CHAPTER 55

Before Danny or Rose had a chance to phone Mary, she surprisingly had gotten in touch with them. Danny wondered if she had somehow learned about what Jack had done, then realized that was impossible. He had made sure the news was kept out of the media.

"I'm coming home," she announced. "Something came up and well, I just want to go home. Live in the states for a while."

"Mary! I was just going to phone you," Danny said. He filled her in on what was happening with Jack. Mary listened to what her son had done to that Timothy person, feeling pride that he would defend his girlfriend's honor like that. And then she heard Danny use the word *schizophrenia* to explain away the incident. How ridiculous. No child Mary bore would be a nutcase! Didn't her father tell her once that Jack's IQ was sky high? Bordering on genius? Yes, he did; several times as she recalled. What a clever excuse for Jack to use for doing the right thing in a world that would want to punish him for what he had done to that lowlife scumbag.

"Is he going to be all right?

"Unfortunately, the boy had to have a partial leg amputation and -

"Jack," she said. "Is *Jack* going to be alright?"

It was the first time she had had every referred to one of the twins by their given name.

"Of course. He's been admitted to *Cliff Manor* in Newport, and receiving excellent care. He'll be happy to have you home, Mary. Jack always pined for you to come back to live with us.

When will you be returning to the states?"

Mary glanced at her packed luggage. "I'm catching the next plane out," she said, sensing she would arrive in time to avoid disaster. Judging by her father's tone she was safe, at least for the moment.

"I'll send my private jet," Danny offered, but Mary thought hopping on a commercial flight would be faster.

"No. No. I want to get home as fast as I can," she told him. "Especially now with what's going on with Jack. I have no time to wait for our jet to arrive."

"Perhaps you're right," Danny agreed. "Well, I'll have Sully pick you up at the airport."

"Can we send for my things in France?" Mary asked. She had decided it best she stay stateside for a while, at least until she could figure out if John Paul would go through with his threat.

"I don't understand. Aren't you *in* France?" Danny asked.

"I'm…I'm visiting a friend in Switzerland, so no."

Danny thought it marvelous that after all the time that had passed, his daughter would abandon a vacation to be at her son's side at his time of need.

"Of course, Mary. Of course," he repeated.

"Well?" Rose said, when Danny hung up.

"Mary's catching the next flight out."

"And we didn't even have to phone her and tell her what happened! She got in touch with us first. That's because of Mary's maternal instinct, you know," Rose said. nodding. "She must have sensed that something was wrong with her son."

Danny, remembering that Rose had no trouble identifying the twins when they were babies said, "Maybe you have a point." Without thinking he reached out and took her hand in his, squeezing it a little.

"This time I hope she stays home for good," Rose said, pleased that her family would once again be together under one roof.

As Danny and Rose discussed the implications of their daughter's return, Mary replaced the receiver thinking that if her parents knew the real reason she was heading for the states, they'd be bullshit. She just prayed she'd get home in time so they didn't have to find out.

Her mind drifted back to John Paul who must have followed her back to her hotel in Switzerland after she had confronted him and that bitch Amelia, because he showed up at her suite the next day as she was planning her revenge.

"Did you come here to fuck me, John Paul?" Mary sneered, but all he said was, "You're the one who will be, as you so aptly put it, fucked. Do you remember Malachi? Probably not, but he fathered your handsome boys. Malachi is back in France right now as we speak preparing to send the video of you and poor, dear Adele to your father."

Mary stepped back, her mind racing, a hand to her throat.

"No one will trace the money you gave to me and my beautiful Amelia," John Paul sneered. I told you to leave us alone, Mary. I *warned* you. You should have listened, but you chose otherwise." John Paul sighed. "Now you have a major problem I'd say. Imagine the surprise on your father's face when he sees for himself what you have been up to in your younger days. And then there's the fact that Adele had been murdered. I think -

"*Shut the fuck up!*" Mary shouted.

She never dreamed that John Paul would really follow through with his black mail threat, especially now after all these years.

"*You're lying, John Paul!*"

"Oh? Well, you're about to find out," He snickered, then turned his back to her, and walked stiffly out the door.

Mary stared after him, not knowing what to do, shaking with rage before the rage turned into fear.

And damn him, he was right. She didn't want to take the chance that he would actually go through with his devious plan. That's when she phoned her parents, praying that she would arrive home in time to prevent her downfall.

*My father will be devastated to see that sex tape*, she thought. *Horrified that I strangled Adele to death. He's a doctor. A man who saves the lives of people, not one who kills them! My father would never hurt a soul*, Mary thought. *He will take me out of his will for what I had done. Even prevent me from accessing my trust money. How will I live then?*

"Oh God. What have I done!" she said aloud, sobbing into her hands.

# CHAPTER 56

Mary arrived at *Hollyberry House* two days later. Her first jet had been delayed at Zurich Airport due to inclement weather, and then during a layover in Germany for an unknown reason, except Mary thought, for the gods being against her.

Sasha, who had been with the Oxman family since Mary was a child, let her inside when Mary finally arrived, exhausted, and hungry.

"Ms. Oxman. It is so nice to have you home! Can I get -

"Has the mail come?"

"The mail?" Sasha said, raising her eyebrows. She was expecting Mary to ask about Jack.

"Yes. You know. The mail. Envelopes, and packages and things?" Mary snapped, unable to hide her sarcasm.

"I don't believe...let me go check," Sasha said, moving away, and then she returned, holding a few envelopes. "Well, these came in the last few days addressed to your parents," she told her.

Mary felt an instant sense of relief, but that feeling quickly vanished when John Paul's words echoed in the cauldron of her mind.

*Malachi is back in France right now as we speak, preparing to send the video of you and poor, dear Adele...*

"I meant a package. A *box*. Not some *fucking* papers," Mary hissed, as Sasha took a step backwards, her eyes wide.

"I'm sorry," Mary said, instantly regretting her tone. "Please understand. I'm just worried about Jack and, well, someone sent something for him through the mail. A special package."

"Oh, well. No. No package," Sasha said. I'll keep an eye out for one, though."

Mary's adrenaline-charged muscles suddenly relaxed, and total exhaustion set in. She desperately wanted to sleep, but she forced herself to ask, "How is my son? My father said he's hospitalized?"

"Cliff Manor in Newport, Rhode Island. Yes. Your parents and brother are still with him now. I...I'll take your luggage to the guest room."

"No. I want to stay in my old bedroom," Mary said, her voice low. "It was where my brother died, you know. I will feel closer to James staying in that room."

Sasha put a hand to her heart. This poor woman, she thought. She lost her brother, and her Uncle Ronnie, who Sasha remembered Mary had been close to as a child. And now Jack was so ill. No one person should live through so much pain.

"Of course. I'll get your room ready," Sasha said. "Right away, ma'am."

When Mary fell into bed a half hour later, she slept for twelve straight hours.

# CHAPTER 57

The next afternoon, Mary took the family's private jet from Boston to Warwick, Rhode Island where she rented a car, then she drove to *Cliff Manor*. Jet lag, combined with the stress of returning to the states in anticipation of what she may find, had taken a toll on her too. She was getting too old, she thought, to be dealing with her past life choices, and now her teenage son's apparent mental illness, which she still didn't believe could be possible.

A woman at the reception desk asked for identification, and then escorted Mary to what she called the Day Room, which looked like a spacious, elegant family room. People mingled everywhere, although it was difficult to tell the visitors apart from the patients, since everyone was dressed in street clothing. Mary wondered how long the patients had to be imprisoned here, but it was a fleeting thought.

"Mary!" Rose exclaimed, pushing herself slowly up from a lounge chair. She hugged her daughter, feeling Mary stiffen against her, but that was understandable. Mary had not been home in a very long time.

For her part, Mary saw how old her mother looked, horrified at the wrinkles etched into her face, and at the sight of her ugly blue veined hands, before she turned and hugged her father tightly, thinking how handsome he still looked, and how well he had aged.

Xavier came over, and proffered his hand.

"Hello, mother," he said.

Mary was shocked at how handsome her son was with his dark

curly hair, and solem gray eyes. She peered at his face closely, trying to see a resemblance to Malachi. She shook his hand. "Jack."

"Xavier," he corrected. "Jack's over there." He pointed to a corner of the room, where Jack had wedged himself.

"Go on, Mary. Say hello," Rose urged.

Mary walked over to the corner, peering into the face of her youngest son. Jack looked exactly like his brother, but there was a blank look in his eyes she could not understand.

"Jack?"

"Brie?" He said, looking up at her with a smile.

Mary turned towards her parents.

"No, Jack. It's your mother," Rose told him.

"I…I don't have a, ah mother," Jack said, and Harry whispered fragmented words – *Old photograph. Night table. Pretty womaaaan.*

"Oh. Right. Harry says you're…my mother."

"Harry? Who's Harry?" Mary asked.

***

The Oxman's stayed at a rented beach house in Newport for the next few weeks, visiting Jack daily. Danny stayed in close contact with his grandson's medical team, monitoring Jack's medications, and discussing further psychiatric treatment with the specialists there. Rose was content that, despite Jack's mental health problems, the family was finally together again. Meanwhile, Xavier worried about his brother, hoping the medication would help him get a grip on his life, while Mary hated everything about *Cliff Manor.* She spent her time there worried that Amelia's package had arrived back at *Hollyberry House*, and was sitting amongst the other mail waiting for her parents to get to it before she could.

Rose was aware of her daughter's depressive state, but understood her distress. Even though Mary hadn't been a major figure in her son's lives, of course she would be worried about Jack at a time like this. Rose was inordinately pleased to see that Xavier was polite to Mary, even though he was aloof towards his mother. That aloofness, she hoped would, ebb over time, now that Mary was going to be living home again.

Finally, during his fourth week of hospitalization, Jack was discharged, a judge mysteriously having dropped the assualt with intent to kill charges filed against him.

"We'll hire a fleet of nurses to care for him at home," Danny announced during a family meeting. "He'll require intensive monitoring, but I believe his medication is working as well as can be expected."

"What does that mean?" Rose asked. She had not been included in the discussions Danny had had with the medical team. The information was too overwhelming for her.

"What does what mean?

"Won't the medication cure him?"

Danny shook his head. "Not entirely, but it's a start," he explained, and Xavier assured both grandparents that he would keep a close eye on his brother.

"I won't let anything happen to him," Xavier promised, and Mary wondered how she could have given birth to such a caring son, as she thought about her own brother, and how James had died.

***

The minute the Oxman's arrived back at *Hollyberry House*, Mary sought out Sasha. "Did the package arrive?"

"No, ma'am."

Mary pressed her lips together, racking a hand through her blonde hair. John Paul had lied to get rid of her! Well, she would need some time to figure out how to deal with him. A vision of her straddling Adele with a purple silk scarf while they were both naked popped into Mary's mind, unbidden. The feelings that followed were disconcerting. Mary decided it best to stay at *Hollyberry House* for a while. There was time enough later for her to deal with John Paul, and that bitch Amelia.

# CHAPTER 58

After their return from *Cliff Manor* Danny declared, "We all need time to decompress. I'm taking a few weeks off, so we can have some family time together. Mary, we can discuss your future plans soon. I would like you to come work for Oxman & Sons, Inc. That will give you something to do."

Mary smiled. "I'm not ready to take over the company, dad, although that would –

"Take over – Danny smiled, patting his daughter's hand. "Of course not, Mary. You can start off as a lab tech in any division you'd like. I'll make sure you have excellent training. Xavier will be attending Harvard in another year, and when he graduates, he'll be promoted. Besides, you should spend most of your time with Jack."

Mary fell speechless, as Xavier smiled over at her.

"I've been interning for grandpa since ninth grade. I enjoy being at Oxman & Sons more than -

Mary stopped listening, her mind whirling. Her only clear thought was how the hell she was going to manage to get away from her family, and back to a sane life in France where she would go through with her plan to properly punish John Paul and Malachi - the father of the twins! – for the wrong they had done to her.

At that moment, Rose walked into the grand room. "I'm sorry Danny, with everything that's been going on I forgot to tell you. This package came just before Mary arrived."

"Oh?" Danny said, raising his eyebrows. "What is it?"

"I don't know. It's addressed to you."

"Who's it from?"

Rose looked over at Mary who forced her mouth not to drop open at this utter surprise. A tangled ball of fear welled inside her chest. She prayed for a heart attack ,and thought maybe now was a good time to fake one.

"The return label gives a Paris address, but it's not yours," Rose said, turning towards Mary with knitted eyebrows. "Perhaps a friend sent it?"

Mary had no words.

"Give it here," Danny said, waving a hand. Rose handed him the box, while Xavier found a sterling silver letter opener, handing it to his grandfather. Mary saw the sharp edge slice through the tan masking tape that bound the seals, thinking how she'd love to slice John Paul's neck open with this very instrument.

"It's a video tape," Danny said, as he pulled out a cassette, scattering tiny balls of green Styrofoam onto the floor as a result. He rooted a hand inside the box, then added, "No note. Do you have any idea who sent this Mary?"

Mary forced herself up from her chair, and glanced at the return address, which was unfamiliar to her, but her first thought was: *Malachi*. She memorized the street number and name.

"No idea," she said truthfully.

Xavier took the video tape from Danny's hands before Mary could stop him.

"Let's see what it is," he said, turning on the television then slipping the tape into the slot, as Mary watched, thinking wildly how to stop him.

Xavier pressed *Play*, then stepped back for a clearer view, as did Rose. Jack sat on the floor staring at the ceiling, oblivious. Mary's eyes were frozen to the screen as the whir of the tape sounded in the stillness of the room; then the television speakers crackled. Mary felt the blood drain from her face.

More gray static, and then images appeared, but they were

grainy, and unrecognizable, disappearing as fast as they had come, followed by a slate of solid black footage. Mary's heart pounded in her ears, but after a full minute of nothing but blackness, Danny said, "I don't understand. Maybe the DVD got demagnetized in the mail," and that's when Mary said, "Excellent point," as the color returned to her cheeks, and Xavier said, "*Damn*. I was hoping for something good."

"Don't say damn," Rose sniffed. "It's not polite."

"Sorry grandma."

Jack looked over at Mary and said, "Harry wants ya to know you're safe now mother," and his words sent a shiver up her spine.

## Epilogue

The Prime Minister of Canada, Corbin Cornell, stood in front of the full-length mirror in his hotel room in Quebec, pulling the knot of his tie closer to his neck before running a hand through wavy silver hair. For a man in his mid-fifties he thought he looked pretty damn good.

A soft knock at the door caught his attention. "Yes?" He called.

"Sir? The conference is about to start."

"Thank you, Albert," Corbin said. "I'll be down in a moment. Tell the Americans they will have to wait."

"Yes, sir."

It was a crisp fall day with hints of winter in the air. Corbin felt the breeze through the open window, the curtains bustling softly. He grabbed his leather wallet from the bureau just as the phone jangled. He glanced at his watch, then picked up the receiver.

"Hello?"

"When will you be home, darling? Benjamin and Jasmine will be here with Bell at three. You can't miss your daughter's sweet sixteen birthday party."

"Of course not," Albert said. "I can sneak out from the conference early. American's are always in a hurry, anyway. I'm sure they'll be delighted to play an early round of golf. Sans me, of course."

"Oh, that's wonderful darling. And I bought some Cuban cigars for you, and Kyle," the woman said.

Corbin chuckled. His wife was always surprising him. "Ah, sounds very good, my dear."

"See you soon, darling."

Corbin hung up.

So did Adele.

*It's chilly*, she thought, moving into the master bedroom that she shared with Corbin, her husband of nearly twenty years. She rummaged for a scarf in a top drawer of a tall bureau, pulling out the long sheath of purple silk, its edges tattered a bit, not that she minded. It was her favorite scarf after all, and she often wore it over the past two decades.

Adele wrapped the soft silk loosely around her neck, then lovingly stroked the material with her finger tips, reminiscing about her younger years, thinking how wild she had been back in the day, and then she tilted her head back, and laughed aloud, pleased that she had been lucky enough to marry the Prime Minister of Canada without him ever finding out about her racy past.